HALF MOON RANCH

RANCH

NAVAHO JOE

Also by Jenny Oldfield
published by Hodder Children's Books

HORSES OF
HALF MOON
RANCH

NAVAHO JOE

JENNY OLDFIELD

Illustrated by
Paul Hunt

Hodder
Children's
Books

a division of Hodder Headline

With thanks to Bob, Karen and Katie Foster, and to the staff and guests at Lost Valley Ranch, Deckers, Colorado and special thanks to the pupils of La Sagesse Junior School, North Jesmond, Newcastle-upon-Tyne.

First published in Great Britain in 2000
by Hodder Children's Books

A Catalogue record for this book is available from the British Library

ISBN 0 340 75727 2

Typeset by Avon Dataset Ltd, Bidford-on-Avon, Warks

Printed and bound in Great Britain by
The Guernsey Press Co. Ltd, Channel Islands

Hodder Children's Books
a division of Hodder Headline
338 Euston Road
London NW1 3BH

1

'No more guests for four whole months!' Sandy Scott sank back in the big leather settee in front of a bright log fire. 'Just think; November through February and not a single dude rider for us to take care of!'

'Yeah, and no money coming in either,' Matt reminded her. He kicked a smouldering log with the heel of his boot so that it settled more firmly into the grate. Sparks flew up the sooty stone chimney, chased by bright orange and yellow flames.

Kirstie listened to her older brother hassle her mom. After a long day riding the trails, she loved the red sparks and the smell of burning pine. There was something satisfying too about the row of wet leather gloves laid out to dry, and a comfort in the twang of taut metal strings as Matt's girlfriend, Lachelle, handed him his guitar.

'Quit complaining,' Lachelle told him. 'Just play us a tune.'

'Later maybe.' Matt gave a bashful shrug and made out he didn't want to be the centre of attention.

Since when? Kirstie thought to herself.

'Please, Mattie!' Lachelle pouted and fluttered her long lashes at him from under fine, arched brows.

'Oh, OK.' He gave in without too much of a fight and laid the guitar across his knee. Strumming, then slowly picking out a tune, he cleared his throat ready to sing.

From her seat by the window, Kirstie smiled at Matt and Lachelle playing their little games. She looked out at the darkening summit of Eagle's Peak on the jagged horizon, and at the patches of white snow already lying above 8,000 feet. Fall was almost over and winter about to begin.

Matt sang in a slow, low, cowboy drawl.

> ' "Ah'm tired of workin' dawn to dusk,
> Long days an' little pay.
> Ah want to work under city lights,
> Big money's th'only way." '

Working dawn till dusk is right! Kirstie thought, letting her mind drift with the music. Living at Half-Moon Ranch meant getting up early, day in, day out, to bring the horses in from Red Fox Meadow. Feed and groom them, saddle them up, lead them and their dude riders out along Five Mile Creek, up to Eden Lake and on again into the high mountains of the Meltwater Range.

'Chorus!' Matt cried.

Sandy sang from the depths of the settee. Lachelle joined in from her perch on the arm of Matt's chair. Hadley Crane and Charlie Miller, the wranglers who had just come in out of the cold, stood in the doorway and hummed.

> ' "Oh let me leave Colorado,
> No more herdin' cows all day,

3

Oh let me leave Colorado,
And I'll be on my-y way!" '

'Oh let me leave Colorado . . .' Kirstie began the first line, then stopped.

No way! she thought, staring out at the moon and stars. *What am I saying*? Who in their right mind would want to move back to Denver or any other city for that matter, after even one spring spent watching the blue columbines flower in the mountains?

Who would willingly change crystal-clear Five Mile Creek for the grot and grunge of the Hudson River? Or the bliss of riding her palomino horse, Lucky, bareback along the shore of Eden Lake for the nose-to-tail gridlock of Brooklyn Bridge?

'You sound like my grandpa!' Kirstie's best friend, Lisa Goodman, would say, any time Kirstie happened to talk this way. 'Wouldn't you like to live some place with shopping malls and movie theatres?'

'Nope,' was Kirstie's stubborn reply. *Been there, got the T-shirt.*

Five years back. Denver. Misery and heartbreak.

'. . . Kirstie, honey.' Sandy's soft voice broke into her thoughts. 'Would you please make hot chocolate for two hard-working wranglers?'

She blinked and shut out the moon and turned back to the bright, warm room and the present.

'Sure thing!' she said. Then, 'Sing something more upbeat,' she told Matt as she headed for the kitchen. 'Sing Rocky Mountain High!'

'It's sure been a hard summer for Sandy,' Hadley said, as he rode out on Moose with Kirstie and Lucky.

It was early next morning. The pre-dawn light was grey, the air still and cold. The two riders were on their way over to Jim Mullins' place to help the neighbouring rancher bring in the last of his cattle left out on the mountain, before the snow came.

'I know it,' Kirstie sighed.

The long summer days of looking after visitors had taken their toll. Just yesterday, as her mom piled the last bunch into the mini-bus to drive them to the airport, the smile on her tanned face had looked faded and strained.

'She gonna take a break?' The old wrangler was

unusually talkative. Silent riding was more Hadley's style; jacket collar turned up, battered stetson pulled well down, worn leather chaps brushing low branches as he picked his way through pine trees on the steep, rocky slopes.

'Come Christmas,' Kirstie told him. She was watching for the gold glimmer in the east that signalled the rising of the sun. Already, after only ten minutes on the trail, her fingers and toes were numb with cold. 'Before that she's gonna build those two new cabins out towards Hummingbird Rock.'

Two new cabins meant eight more paying guests for next season. Matt had done the arithmetic and said it was a sound investment, so they planned to go ahead with the work.

'I've been thinking about taking a break myself.' Hadley let his sturdy grey quarter horse pick his way up Meltwater Trail.

This was the first Kirstie had heard of it. She clicked her tongue to urge Lucky on and catch him up. 'What kind of a break?'

'A good long one. I'm sixty-five come February. I've been on the ranch well nigh forty years, when your grandpa and grandma were just starting up.'

'Hey, are we talking retirement here?' The idea shocked and unsettled her. Half-Moon Ranch without Hadley was too weird to contemplate.

'Maybe.' He reined Moose to the right, across a shallow, fast-running stream. The horse splashed through without hesitating, but going up the far bank, he lost his footing and stumbled. Hadley righted the horse. 'We're getting long in the tooth, me and Moose both,' he admitted to Kirstie. 'Maybe it's time I hung up my boots.'

Kirstie glanced at the battered boots poking out from under the chaps. The pointed toes curled up, the tan leather was scuffed and creased, the edges of the heels worn down. Like the old wrangler's lined, weatherbeaten face, they'd seen better days. 'Did you say anything to Mom yet?'

Hadley nodded.

'What did she say?'

'She said to think about it before I made my final decision.'

'But ranch work is all you've got!' Kirstie didn't need to remind Hadley of the years spent cutting and roping cattle, of coming out like this before

7

it was daylight, saddling up his horse and riding the lonely trail. Still, the protest against such a huge change just slipped out.

Hadley rode head down, shoulders hunched, along the narrow ledge of Miners' Ridge. Old Moose strode on, surefooted again after his momentary stumble. 'Yeah,' he sighed. 'I've been a cowboy all my life.'

The sun came up between the pine trees, their trunks like tall black columns, their canopies of intertwined branches letting glimmers of light fall on the frosty ground.

'Two bovines over on Elk Pass,' Jim Mullins had reported before he sent Kirstie and Hadley up there to bring them in. 'Aberdeen Angus cow and calf. They cut off from a bunch we rounded up last night, headed into a stand of aspens where we couldn't reach 'em. I reckon they'll still be in there somewhere.'

Hadley had said he knew the place. It involved back-tracking to Miners' Ridge, then climbing a couple of hundred feet to a small plateau. He told Kirstie that Jim's two runaway cows would have chosen the spot because it was sheltered from the wind and there would still be grass to graze.

'It's pretty lonely up there,' he warned. 'There's nothing but mountain between Elk Pass and Coyote Cow Station over the east side of Eagle's Peak.'

Prepared for a long ride, Kirstie was glad to see the sun. There was no warmth in it yet, as it filtered through the pine branches, but at least it brought colour to the hillside. It made the pink granite sparkle under the horses' feet and turned the scaly bark of the ponderosa pines a patchy, rusty red.

Even Moose's dull grey coat took on a sheen in the sun's rays, she noticed, and Lucky's smooth neck and shoulders turned the colour of new gold. Her palomino, her friend, her Lucky.

Smooth, even steps up the mountain. A gentle swaying in the saddle. The creak of stirrup leathers. Lucky flicking his ears this way and that.

'Bovines!' Hadley's sharp call snapped her out of her contented daydream. He and Moose stood on a ridge, looking down into the next culvert.

Click! Kirstie urged her horse into a trot and then a lope. By the time she reached the ridge, fifty yards up the hill, the wrangler had already started to descend into the sheltered valley. From above, she saw the top of his white stetson, Moose's broad grey back, and beyond them a flash of orange-red amongst the silvery white of the slender aspen trees.

'I'll try and cut 'em off from beyond the stand of trees!' she yelled at Hadley. Her plan was to get behind the two cows and drive them towards the wrangler, who would be waiting with his lasso. If he could rope the calf and lead her back to Lazy B, then the mother would surely follow.

So she raced along the ridge, trying to keep Hadley in her sights, but losing him amongst the trees. Now she must find a place to cut right off the high ground and plunge into the culvert. This was easier said than done, she found, since the ground fell steeply from the ridge and there was no soft, safe footing for Lucky to take.

'Yip-yip-yip!' Way below, Hadley's voice roused the grazing cattle.

The muffled cry rose up the sides of the narrow valley, disturbing a chipmunk which had been hiding under a log by Lucky's hooves. The small, striped creature shot out into the open, its bushy tail held high, darting across a lichen-covered rock and vanishing under a root.

Lucky skittered sideways, then took the decision to crash boldly through undergrowth on a downward track. His feet trampled pine cones and snapped through twigs, raising other small, frightened animals.

'Yip!' Hadley called from below, flushing out the bovines from their refuge amongst the aspens.

'Easy!' Kirstie whispered.

Lucky's head went up and he shook his pale mane. For a moment he lost his balance and slid a few feet through pine needles and soft mud. Kirstie lurched forward in the saddle and grabbed the horn, losing her cap as it knocked against an overhead branch.

'Jeez!' she breathed. The denim cap lay on the ground behind them, so she had to make a quick dismount to retrieve it. When she went back to Lucky, flicking the cap against her thigh to knock off the dirt, she found him still edgy. 'Take it easy,' she told him, sliding her foot into the broad stirrup. Then she heaved herself on to his back, ready to make another attempt to join Hadley and Moose down below.

She clicked and gave Lucky's flanks a small kick with her heels.

Instead of walking on, he stood and listened, ears forward, straining his neck.

'C'mon!' Kirstie insisted. At this rate, they would be too late to help drive the cows out of the culvert.

But Lucky was stubborn. He looked, he listened, but he didn't move a muscle.

And then Kirstie saw why. There was a movement on the opposite ridge and for a moment she thought the crafty cattle must have climbed out of the valley on a track only they knew. Branches swayed, bushes rustled as the creatures emerged on to the high ground.

Or perhaps only one creature. Kirstie looked more closely. From her first glimpse, she saw that the animal was big enough to be a cow, but paler and less red than an Aberdeen Angus. Maybe it was a mule deer or an elk. She studied the bushes for a sight of antlers.

They didn't appear. Instead, she caught a glimpse of a sleek neck and head through the latticework of branches. The creature was mainly white with dark brown markings, like flecks of paint speckling a pale background.

Lucky flared his nostrils as the animal made it to the ridge and appeared in all his glory. He threw back his head and gave a shrill cry.

The newcomer turned to look. His head was held high, his neck was arched. The powerful, curved back was tilted downwards on to the haunches, as if ready to rear up.

'Appie!' Kirstie whispered. She had time to make out the pattern of brown against cream, the flick of a long white tail. An Appaloosa. The horse stood above fifteen hands; its muscle solid as rock, its legs long and graceful, its eyes wild.

Lucky shrilled out a greeting from ridge to ridge; the deep, frosty culvert between. One horse staking out its territory, saying to the other, 'Here I am!'

The Appaloosa went up on its hind legs. Its front hooves pawed the air. It landed, wheeled away and began to run the ridge; higher into the mountain, towards the snowline and the low-hanging clouds.

'Come back!' Kirstie called. She'd spotted a

headcollar, a snapped lead-rope snaking through the air as the horse reared.

The Appie gathered speed. He loped amongst pines, weaving in and out, hooves thundering on rock. He was there, then he was gone.

After a while, as Kirstie held her breath and screwed up her eyes to see, he reappeared higher up the mountain, crossing a patch of recently fallen snow. He was still visible against the pure white background, but ghostly now; a phantom flitting soundlessly across the frozen hillside.

Was he real?

'Come back!' she whispered to the magnificent horse.

Was he lost?

The Appaloosa kicked up snow into a cloud of white dust that sparkled in the sunlight.

Soon he would be gone for good. Kirstie kicked Lucky into action and began to sprint after him. She raced up her ridge to the point where the culvert came to a head and joined the Appie's ridge; then on up the mountain.

As Lucky's hooves hit the bank of snow, all sound was deadened and Kirstie entered a vast, white, silent world.

2

Kirstie and Lucky made it across the snowdrift on to a stretch of dirt track.

The Elk Pass route was kept clear by Smiley Gilpin and his small team of forest guards using a big yellow snow-mover. The only road through to the far side of Eagle's Peak, it was important to keep it open so that the ranchers in the Meltwater foothills could truck out the last of their cattle to San Luis and beyond. Come December though, when the thick, whirling Rocky Mountain blizzards set in, there was no way that anyone could get through.

Her horse's hooves hit dirt and thundered on. Lucky's breathing came short and fast, he was blowing heavily. From below, Hadley called her back.

But the only thing on Kirstie's mind was the lost horse.

That's what she called the Appie from the moment she saw him: the lost horse. She caught a second fleeting glimpse of his ghostly shape brushing through trees, bringing showers of heavy snow down from the branches. He was galloping without direction, his mane and tail flying back, fleeing as though his life depended on it.

'Kirstie!' Hadley appeared on the track some four or five hundred yards behind, beyond a series of sharp hairpin bends.

'Lost horse!' she yelled, loping on.

So he and Moose set off to follow, and though the grey horse was old, he was fresher than Lucky and began to make up ground.

The Appaloosa, though, began to surge ahead. He carried no weight of saddle or rider, he was strong and athletic with heavy hind-quarters that gave him a burst of speed; the perfect Native American mustang. Kirstie could picture him long ago on the wide prairies in a sea of silver-green grass. He would carry a bare-chested rider in buckskin trousers. The brave's black hair would be braided; he would be Shawnee, Comanche or Navaho. Navaho Joe; that was the name she would have given the strong-willed runaway horse.

At least he's no ghost! she thought grimly. She could see the lead-rope whipping back against his neck, could hear the even beat of shod hooves on the track. *He's real and, if you ask me, he doesn't know where he's headed*!

Suddenly, without warning, the runaway horse reached yet another bend and veered off the track. He plunged up to his belly into a snowdrift, struggled to lift his legs, then floundered helplessly.

'C'mon, Lucky!' This was their chance! As the palomino gave her his last ounce of strength, she reached down to untie the coil of rope attached to her saddle horn. When she got close, she would raise the lasso over her head, aim for the Appaloosa and rope him in.

The Appie heard them approach. Eyes rolling

wildly, he dug himself deeper into the snow. It caked his flanks and clung to his mane in icy chunks.

Kirstie and Lucky drew level. The lasso was circling around her head when Hadley shouted a warning.

'Get off the road!' he yelled. 'Truck comin'!'

Her arm jerked and she misthrew. The loop of rope landed wide. Meanwhile, Lucky backed away and the Appaloosa at last found firm ground under his feet. He pulled himself clear of the drift.

A truck's engine roared and ground its way up the hill. As Kirstie gathered in her rope and tried to steady her horse, it appeared round the bend, overtaking Hadley and Moose, churning up a mixture of mud and dirty snow. A big red monster of a truck with silver fenders and grille, the giant vehicle trundled and throbbed towards her, dragging behind it a trailer loaded with fifty-foot pine poles.

'Easy, Lucky. Easy, boy!' Kirstie had to use all her concentration and skill to hold her horse steady. The smell of diesel, the flash of sunlight against the silver grille unnerved him and made him bunch his muscles tight. She backed him off the track, down a safe, shallow gulley from where they could watch the truck crawl by.

It seemed to take an age for the load of logs to pass. She could see Hadley holding Moose back, a hundred yards behind the truck, but for as long as it took the giant vehicle to drive past, she could catch no sight of the lost Appaloosa. She just had to hope and pray that the horse would still be there, and willing now to be brought down to the nearby Lazy B.

She already had plans for Navaho Joe. They included a good feed in a warm barn, a message sent out to the neighbouring ranches that a lost horse had been found. Before long, someone would call Jim back and claim the Appie. There would be thanks all round. Joe would soon be home with his owner.

The timber-truck took the bend at a snail's pace; huge black wheels kicking up stones and snow as they skimmed the very edge of the track. Kirstie heard a wild whinny from the Appie; expected to see him huddled against a rock once the nightmare truck had passed, waiting for rescue.

At last the road was clear. Hadley was trotting

Moose forward to join her as Lucky climbed out of the gulley. They reached the track and she looked across to the drift, at the churned up mess where the runaway horse had fallen into the snow.

'So, what exactly are we talking about here?' Hadley said, tipping his hat back and staring at the empty landscape.

'The Appaloosa!' Kirstie gasped. There were tracks, but no horse. In the time it had taken the truck to roll by, Navaho Joe had vanished.

'I don't see no Appie!' the old wrangler said with a puzzled frown. He gazed up the mountain, then down the pass.

'But he was here!' Kirstie protested. 'He was lost. I saw him on the ridge, then he loped up this way; those are his tracks!'

'Sure.' Hadley shrugged and pulled up the needlecord collar of his green-checked woollen jacket.

'Don't you believe me? Didn't you hear him call?'

'I heard Lucky, but I didn't hear no lost horse.'

Kirstie teetered on the edge of the messed-up drift, eyes raking the hillside, listening out for more telltale sounds. But none came. A wind whistled down from Eagle's Peak, raising a fine powder of snow that blew in their faces and coated the horses in a sparkling white dust. The powder covered Joe's tracks, smoothed them out and made it seem as if he'd never existed.

'C'mon,' Hadley said when he'd given Kirstie time to convince herself that she must have made a mistake. 'Let's go find us some bovines!'

'*I* believe you!' Lisa told Kirstie late on Sunday afternoon. She'd been at Half-Moon Ranch since midday, waiting for her friend to return.

The cow and calf had been cornered in the culvert and taken back to the Lazy B; the very last of Jim's cattle to be brought down. Kirstie had mentioned the lost horse to the ranch hands there; had anyone seen a runaway Appie over by Elk Pass? Had any worried owner been out this way to look?

Nope. The wranglers at Mullins' place had shrugged it off. If there was a horse loose up there they sure would've heard. Anyhow, if Kirstie was right, the critter would soon come down off the mountain for food and shelter. Snow was forecast. Winter was setting in.

'How come Hadley didn't see it?' Matt asked, setting Kirstie's gloves and boots to dry by the fire. Lachelle had gone home to San Luis and he was in no mood for his kid sister's romantic fantasies.

'He couldn't see because he was down in the culvert rounding up cattle!' Kirstie explained in an exasperated voice. 'By the time he arrived, the Appie had escaped!'

'Yeah!' Lisa defended her friend's version. She loved a mystery and a drama. 'You guys want answers to everything. Why can't it be a runaway, escaping from cruel owners, fighting to stay free?'

Matt sighed and set another log on the fire. 'Yeah, very Hollywood!' he scoffed. 'The fact is, it ain't natural for a horse to stay out there all alone in this weather. Horses are herd animals – if one breaks loose and gets lost up a mountain, the first thing it does is make its way to the nearest ranch to join some others.'

'This one didn't,' Kirstie muttered. When Lucky had called out across the culvert, the Appie had taken off in the opposite direction.

'So, he stays out in the freezing cold; no food, nothing. He does exactly the opposite of what it takes to survive!' Matt was squaring up to her, ready for a row. 'Like I say, it ain't natural.'

'Hey, you guys!' Their mom broke in with news that supper was ready. She gave Kirstie a look that said, 'Quit it. Matt's got a lot on his mind!'

So they went into the big kitchen and sat around the table for steak and fries.

'. . . And how come no one's out there looking?' Matt stabbed a piece of meat with his fork and hassled Kirstie over her far-fetched story of the lost Appaloosa. 'If any horse of mine went missing, I'd sure be out there looking before the snow got serious!'

'Matt!' Sandy warned.

'Maybe the owner *is* looking,' Lisa put in. She wrinkled her snub nose, then gave Matt a wide stare. 'Who knows how far this horse has travelled since he ran off? It could be weeks back. Maybe he's wandered way off his home territory!'

'The lead-rope looked pretty old and worn.' Kirstie picked up on a detail that would fit in with this theory.

Matt rattled his fork on to his plate. 'Maybe . . . maybe!'

'OK, enough!' Sandy had had it. 'Girls, will you please finish your meal and go upstairs to do that schoolwork Lisa brought across?'

'. . . *I* believe you!' Lisa said again, in the privacy of Kirstie's room.

'I'm not crazy, I did see him!' Kirstie felt cut up about the whole thing; her failure to catch Joe and bring him to safety, the fact that no one except Lisa seemed to be interested.

And Kirstie was changing her mind about how the lone horse had come to be on Elk's Pass. In this version there was no worried owner, no warm barn waiting.

'Picture this,' she suggested, gazing out of the window in the dusky half-light and across the red roofs of the tack-room and the barn to Red Fox Meadow, where the Half-Moon Ranch horses took hay from metal feeders. Beyond the meadow, wooded green slopes rose to the snow line, topped by jagged white peaks. 'Say Navaho Joe is a long way from home, like we said. His ranch is hundreds of miles away . . .'

'Maybe not *hundreds*,' Lisa murmured from her position on the spare bed. She lay on her back, hands behind her head, staring up at the sloping, wood-panelled ceiling.

'Whatever.' Kirstie was eager to pursue her theory. 'By now his owners have given up on him. No one's seen him. They think he's dead.'

'Yeah?' This time, Lisa didn't sound so convinced.

'He travels solo over the mountains, keeping out of sight, feeding in hidden meadows, drinking from lakes and streams. Summer turns to fall.'

'Poor guy!' Travelling alone was the idea that touched Lisa's heart. 'It must have been tough.'

'There are bears up on Eagle's Peak, and mountain lions. He doesn't get much sleep nights, and by day he has to move on.'

'Epic!' Lisa whispered.

'The first snow falls. By now he's used to being alone. He doesn't trust anyone. He can't come down to a ranch because there are guys around, and too many other horses. So what does he do for food?'

'I guess he starves.' During the time Kirstie was developing her theory, Lisa had sat up, then stood and came to the window to join Kirstie. She shivered as she looked out at a new moon rising over the mountains.

'Unless someone rescues him!' Kirstie breathed.

'And finds his owner and takes him home?'

There was a long pause. For a moment, Kirstie pictured a ghostly horse in the moonlight, a bareback rider, a bank of pure white snow. 'Or wins his trust and keeps him,' she said. 'Because this is the horse nobody wants!'

3

Night-time was for dreaming. Navaho Joe loped through Kirstie's subconscious; a silent, noble creature with a flowing mane. He was on a mountain-top, across a clear blue lake. He was racing through a green valley; powerful and free.

But Monday morning was wake-up time.

The clouds over the mountains looked grey and heavy with snow and there was a cold mist rolling down the valley.

'Get real,' Matt told her, not unkindly despite the argument of the day before. 'Even if you catch your Appie, we don't have space for him in the ramuda.'

Her Appie. If only!

She nodded as he stopped the pick-up at the end of the five mile dirt road that led from the ranch to Route 5. The San Luis school bus was already rolling towards them, so she only had time for a quick reply as she grabbed her bag of books from behind the seat. 'I know, Matt. Thanks for the ride.'

The yellow bus trundled alongside and jerked to a halt. Kids greeted her as she climbed on board; someone made space on the back seat.

'Thanks!' Kirstie sat down with a sigh, dumping the heavy bag between her feet. She wiped a clear patch in the steamed-up window, gave Matt a wave as he turned the pick-up and headed back to the ranch, then settled in for the fifteen mile drive into town.

Back to reality. There was an exercise for maths which she had to finish before 9.30, an end-of-unit test in science after lunch. So she pulled out a couple of books and tried to work.

But the page of isosceles triangles played tricks on her eyesight. The geometric shapes turned into horses' heads, and the hum of voices on the bus faded as thundering hooves took over.

Kirstie turned her head from the page to gaze out of the window, through the trickles of condensation. The white cone of Eagle's Peak was only half visible through the gloomy clouds. That was where Joe was; somewhere in those deep ravines.

Science! She tried a second book and opened it at a page showing a pencil drawing of the reproductive system of a female ground squirrel.

Ground squirrels made her think of chipmunks, which reminded her of the creature which had shot out from under the log when she first spotted Joe. And then the lost Appaloosa filled her head again, and Matt's voice warning her that it wasn't natural for a horse to stay out there all alone in this weather.

As if to prove his point, when Kirstie glanced out of the window again, she saw that light snowflakes were beginning to fall. Thin and half-hearted, they drifted lazily down and melted the moment they touched the ground. But those were big clouds over the Peak, and the wind was blowing from the west, off the high peaks called the fourteeners in the heart of the Rockies.

'If the snow comes in to the right of Eagle's Peak, there's gonna be a whiteout,' Kirstie's grandpa used to predict. 'If it comes in to the left, you ain't got a problem.'

Left or right? She peered out of the bus to try to judge whether the snowfall was likely to be serious. Both! In fact, the snow was coming in from all directions, and already beginning to thicken. She thought of how it must be up there on Elk Pass, then straightaway tried not to think about it.

Triangles . . . reproductive systems . . . Joe. She juggled images as the bus swayed into town.

It stopped at last at the school gates and fifty kids piled into the yard.

'Hey!' Lisa greeted Kirstie and walked into the school building with her. 'Any more news on Navaho Joe?'

'Nope.' Plenty of dreams and fears; no news.

'I talked to Mom about him when I got back last night.' They were walking down the corridor to the girls' locker room. Metal doors were opening and slamming shut, there was a buzz of talk about the weekend just gone. Lisa said hi to half a dozen kids, then came back to the subject that Kirstie couldn't shake off. 'She had a great idea.'

'Yeah?' Kirstie frowned as she slid her bag into her locker. Lisa's mom, Bonnie Goodman, ran a diner at the end of the town's main street. She was a friendly, busy type, who knew a lot of people through her job.

'Sure. She said it was a shame for the horse to be lost, what with the snow and all, so why didn't we help find his owner?' Lisa pulled out a mirror and combed through her short, wavy red hair.

'Yeah!' Kirstie glanced over Lisa's shoulder at her own untidy, fair mane. She pushed it back behind her ears without much attention to detail. 'How does she plan to do that?'

'We have a noticeboard in the diner,' Lisa reminded her. The locker room was emptying out as kids headed for lessons.

'I know it.' Kirstie always read through the notices and picked out the ones to do with horses. There might be an ad for a new smith in town, or for a guy who made and sold hand-worked saddles, alongside houses and trailers for rent.

'Well, Mom made out a card about the lost

horse.' Lisa smiled up at Kirstie as they went out into the corridor. Kirstie was almost four inches taller; skinnier and lighter. 'She did it real nice; wrote the "Lost horse" part in fancy upper-case, then gave a description of the Appie, together with the place he was last seen.'

'Why didn't you call me?' Kirstie demanded, stopping in her tracks.

'What for? I know what Joe looks like: fifteen hands, brown spots on a white background, mustang type. You told me about him so many times I felt I'd been there!'

'And your mom put the card up in the diner already?' Kirstie felt the blood rush to her face, an unreasonable wave of irritation behind it.

'Sure. It says for anyone who might have lost an Appaloosa in the last few weeks to get in touch with us for more information.' Following Kirstie as she set off angrily down the corridor, Lisa put out a hand to stop her. 'What did we do?'

Kirstie stopped again and turned on her friend. 'What did you do? You only gave every single guy on the street out there a chance to come in with a bunch of lies, saying they own Joe, when really they never set eyes on him in their entire lives!'

'B-but!' The idea hadn't occurred to Lisa. 'Why would anyone do that?'

'Because an Appie's worth money! It's the most popular type of horse next to a paint. And if a cowboy wants to make a quick buck, he'll move in real fast and claim he's Joe's owner, go up the mountain and get a hold of him, then truck him out to the nearest sale barn!' It was so obvious to Kirstie that she could hardly summon the patience to spell it out to her friend.

'Hey!' Lisa's face fell, her whole body sagged. 'Jeez, I'm sorry!'

'. . . Kirstie, Lisa, get a move on. Class begins in thirty seconds!' Miss Stewart, the math teacher, hustled them along.

Kirstie sighed. 'Forget it,' she mumbled. It really wasn't Lisa and Bonnie's fault. They'd done it to help.

But it didn't. It wouldn't. It couldn't. Sitting at her desk, staring blankly at her geometry book, thinking of the big, bold notice on the board in the End of Trail Diner, Kirstie knew she had to move fast.

First she must call Bonnie to explain, then get her to take the sign down. Then she needed to make a new plan and for the snow to ease. The plan could involve alfalfa or oats maybe. She would put it into operation tonight, before it grew dark.

Kirstie decided that alfalfa was best, as she pushed a flap of the sweet-smelling hay into a saddle-bag and strapped it behind Lucky's saddle. It weighed less. She needed plenty of it too, to spread on the ground in Elk Pass; enough to tempt Navaho Joe out of hiding while she lay in wait.

'Let me check your cinch,' Hadley said after she climbed into the saddle. He pulled the strap a couple of holes tighter and handed over a two-way radio for her to carry.

'Was that Mom's idea?' Kirstie glanced across the empty corral towards the ranch house where Sandy was sitting at her desk working out building costs for the two new cabins. The truck that had scared off Navaho Joe on the mountain road had been on its way to Half-Moon Ranch to deliver a stack of timber. This now lay in the yard, covered in a giant yellow tarpaulin, under a light dusting of snow.

'Yup,' Hadley admitted. 'She's kinda worried about you riding out alone.'

'No need.' Zipping her padded jacket to the chin and pulling on her gloves, Kirstie looked up at the clear sky. 'They didn't forecast more snow, did they?'

'Nope.' The wrangler stood aside. 'But the boss wants you back here before six-thirty.'

That meant hard riding all the way. 'Do you reckon I've got enough hay for the Appie?' she asked.

'I guess.' Hadley was back to his one- or two-word answers. He turned and reached to untether Moose from a nearby post. 'C'mon, old fellah, I got a bunch of oats waiting for you.'

'Hey, Hadley!' Kirstie had set off towards the narrow bridge over Five Mile Creek, but recalling their conversation during the round-up, she reined Lucky back for a last word with the old cowboy. 'Did you make a decision yet?'

He paused, lead-rope in hand, turned and shook his head. 'Nope,' he murmured. Then he patted Moose's neck and headed for the barn.

* * *

Kirstie spread the dried alfalfa on the ridge by the culvert where she'd first seen Joe.

She was in a world changed by snow which lay three or four inches deep on trees and rocks. It painted a thin white layer over the landscape, softened edges, killed sound. Sun, which had broken through the cloud around midday, had caused the snow to melt slowly and drip from the branches, then sundown had brought back the freeze. The drips had formed long, thin, clear icicles, which Lucky snapped with his teeth and sucked as Kirstie laid out the hay.

'This'll bring Navaho Joe running,' she told her palomino, leading him out of sight behind a rounded boulder twenty yards away. It was a trick the ranchers used to bring in cows who straggled behind the main herd; when food was short in late fall, the alfalfa was a treat which no animal could resist.

So she settled against the rock to wait, guessing that in five to ten minutes, the wary mustang would have picked up what was going on.

'He's up there somewhere,' she whispered, gazing up the pass, worried by the blue-black cloud gathering on Eagle's Peak.

Nothing between here and the cow station on the far side of the mountain was what Hadley had said; and a cow station was little more than an open-sided barn used to corral cattle when wranglers wanted to brand and process the season's calves. At this time of year it would provide little shelter and no food. The wind would whistle through it, the snow would blow in, so even if the lost horse had found the barn, there would be nothing to keep him there.

'Yep,' Kirstie said to herself, punching a fist into her palm to keep her fingers warm inside her leather gloves. 'He's up there watching us, testing if it's safe to come and take the hay.'

She and Lucky had the patience to wait for him. Joe would have spotted the fresh, dark clouds and know that they would bring snow before morning. He would be cold and hungry. *Not long now*, she promised herself, edging round the boulder to take a look, rope at the ready.

'Hey!' she whispered, one hand on Lucky's neck to keep him back. She'd seen a branch sway fifty yards up the ridge and heard a soft thud of snow fall to the ground. The branch sprang back to reveal an animal creeping stealthily towards the feed.

Then a second and a third. They were big creatures, grey and shadowy amongst the trees, moving clumsily along the ridge, their feet sinking deep into the snow. After a few steps which brought them clear of the stand of lodgepole pines, the leader raised his head and bellowed.

'Elk!' Kirstie's heart sank. There was no mistaking the heavy, spreading antlers of the eight foot male, or the deep, whistling challenge. A female and her half-grown fawn waded through the churned-up snow in his wake, their brown winter coats thick and shaggy, their ears and noses twitching.

From behind the boulder, Lucky breathed out hard with a snort.

The three deer stopped, waited, listened. They weighed up the danger presented by the two hidden intruders into their snowy wilderness, against their sharp hunger. The alfalfa lay twenty paces along the ridge. Should they? Shouldn't they?

Hunger won out.

The big male bellowed a second challenge, shaking his matted reddish-brown mane, crashing his antlers against a tree trunk. Then he kept on coming, followed by the doe and fawn, intent on quickly reaching the alfalfa and gorging themselves.

Kirstie watched helplessly as, almost unable to believe their luck, the deer snatched at the hay intended for the lost horse. They chewed and swallowed greedily, grabbed and chewed some more. Within a couple of minutes, the trampled ground was bare.

'. . . And who can blame them?' Sandy said at supper that evening.

Kirstie and Lucky had returned empty-handed from Elk Pass. The moon was up, the clouds over the mountain still holding off.

The deer had eaten their fill and carried on their winter migration to the lowlands.

Back at the ranch, there was still no word of Navaho Joe, according to Charlie and Hadley, who had been talking with Jim Mullins and the forest rangers. The rancher had hardly been able to believe that any horse would be up there above the snow line, but still he would order his men to keep a lookout. Smiley Gilpin had promised the same thing.

'He said not to hold your breath,' Charlie told Kirstie as she finished her meal and went wearily upstairs to her room. 'Smiley rated his chances of surviving another night at fifty-fifty; less if it snows.'

'Do you want the good news or the bad news?' Lisa asked Kirstie next morning. Kirstie's school bus had been late because of ice on the road. Lisa was waiting in the locker room.

'The good.' Another night of sleep broken by worry about Joe had made her feel sluggish and jaded.

'OK. Mom understood what you were saying about her "Lost Horse" notice, so she took it down.' Lisa waited for Kirstie's reaction, nervously biting the inside of her lip.

'Thanks.' Without looking Lisa's way, Kirstie put her bag in her locker. 'What's the bad news?'

'We took a call from Mineville.'

'And?' Mineville was an old gold-mining town about fifty miles to the south of San Luis. Its gold-rush past had turned it into a tourist trap of souvenir shops and old-style saloon bars. There was a famous steam locomotive that ran along the old narrow-guage track into the mountains where the panhandlers had first struck gold. But Kirstie couldn't for the life of her see what the place had to do with Navaho Joe.

'It was a guy called Ed Fraser. He and his brother run the Buckaroos Trading Post; a clothes store off the interstate highway.' Lisa stopped to bite her lip again.

'So? What did he say? Something about Joe?'

'Maybe.' Still evading the question, Lisa walked between the rows of lockers, out into the corridor.

Kirstie followed her and took a guess. 'Give it to me straight; he claims Joe belongs to them!'

'Yeah. They lost an Appie from outside their store eight weeks back. From his description, it sure sounded like the same horse.'

Mineville? A clothes store? An interstate? 'You have to be joking!' Kirstie laid a hand on Lisa's arm.

Lisa gave an embarrassed shrug.

'But Mineville's fifty miles from here!' Pathetic,

really; Kirstie knew that to a horse like Joe, the distance was nothing.

'Face it,' Lisa said quietly. 'Ed and Jerry Fraser are claiming Joe belongs to them.'

'No way! It's some other horse they lost; not Joe!' Kirstie followed Lisa down the crowded corridor, her incredulous voice lost in the hubbub of noise. 'Joe doesn't belong to a couple of guys who run a store in town. I mean, it's not possible! I just don't believe it!'

4

Come Tuesday afternoon, a big freeze had set in, turning the roads into skating-rinks and sending the kids home early from school.

'The weather stations are predicting nine inches of snow in the next twenty-four hours,' Matt told Kirstie when he picked her up from the bus on Route 5. 'Hadley's getting the snow-mover out of storage and filling her up with diesel. Charlie, me and Mom brought the horses in from Red Fox Meadow. It's gonna be a whiteout like you've never seen!'

'Any news of Navaho Joe?' It was the only question on Kirstie's mind as they took the winding track home. Already, the wind was shifting the existing snow, banking it up at the sides of the track, blowing it hard against the pick-up's windshield.

'Hey, yeah; Charlie mentioned something about him,' Matt said casually, flipping on the wipers, straining to see the road ahead.

'What?' The reply brought Kirstie to the edge of her seat.

'He rode out on Rodeo Rocky earlier today, checking fences up near Miners' Ridge. He thinks he saw your Appie.'

'You see!'

Her yell practically sent Matt swerving into a hidden ditch. Two wheels tipped over the edge, the pick-up skidded and swerved back on track. 'Jeez, Kirstie!'

'If Charlie saw him, it means two things . . . one: I'm not crazy, there really is an Appie up there. And two: he's still alive!'

'Not tonight!' Sandy had insisted when Kirstie jumped out of the pick-up and ran to ask if she could ride out to Elk Pass with more alfalfa.

'But, Mom . . . !'

'You see that sky!' She'd pointed to a bank of heavy grey clouds lurking behind the mountains. 'That means nine inches of snowfall before morning!'

And she'd refused point-blank all Kirstie's pleas on behalf of the lost horse. She'd hurried off to discuss with Hadley which sections of road they should try to keep clear once the snow began, sending Kirstie indoors to check the latest weather reports for herself.

The blizzard lived up to all expectations. It blew in at six-thirty on Tuesday evening and lasted until dawn on Wednesday, clogging the track into the ranch and making it impossible for Kirstie to get out on to the main road to meet the school bus.

'Hadley's been out with the snow-mover since four this morning,' Sandy told Kirstie at breakfast. 'But as soon as he clears a stretch, a whole load more snow comes down and blocks it again.'

'No school for Kirstie!' Matt grinned.

'No college for Matt!' she shot back, her mouth full of waffle drowned in maple syrup.

Wednesday was a big day of the week for her brother's veterinary course.

'Come out and help feed the horses, do something useful,' he suggested, flipping the ponytail which she wore high on her head.

'Mmm. Eatin' breakfast!' she mumbled, pointing to her pouched cheeks. A cold gale and a flurry of snow blew in from the porch as Matt opened the door.

'Charlie's about to take over from Hadley and drive the snow-mover up Meltwater Trail, see if he can clear a way through Elk Pass.' He dropped the piece of information in a laid-back way, watching her reaction over his shoulder, then stepping aside as Kirstie grabbed her jacket and shot out after him. 'We got more timber for the new cabins due in before the end of the week,' he explained.

Kirstie cannoned into Hadley on the porch step, bounced off him and kept on running. She was floundering knee-deep in drifting snow, waving both arms and yelling at Charlie in the cab of the giant yellow snow-mover. Its diesel engine puffed out blue smoke; its caterpillar tracks rolled forward.

'Charlie, Charlie, wait for me!' she yelled, jacket flapping open, boots full of snow, cheeks stinging in the bitter cold. 'Just let me grab a bag of oats from the barn!'

The young, dark-haired wrangler leaned out of the cab, holding a canvas sack. 'No need; I already did!'

So she swerved back across the yard and jumped in alongside him.

'Guess who for?' Charlie tucked the bag between his feet, then slid the snow-mover into forward drive.

'For Joe!' she sighed, settling into the shiny black seat, eagerly watching for signs that the snow was easing. She hoped that soon they would be able to see their way along the trail through the mesmerizing, swirling white flakes.

'Matt tells me you saw Joe,' Kirstie checked with the young wrangler as they rumbled along the side of Five Mile Creek.

The huge metal scoop on the front of the machine pushed the snow aside and left behind a curiously patterned, flattened trail. To their right, the water in the creek was frozen over and the ice hidden beneath a deep blanket of snow.

'Yesterday, about three in the afternoon.'

'How did he look?'

'Not so good. Lord knows what he's finding to eat up there.' Concentrating hard, Charlie turned across a concrete bridge, built ten years earlier by the forest rangers, to give logging trucks an easier route up to Elk Pass.

Kirstie pressed for more information on Joe. 'Did he see you? What did he do?'

'Sure, he saw us. Rocky let him know we were there, and for a couple of minutes I thought the Appie was gonna come off the ridge to meet us.'

'Just like me and Lucky,' Kirstie agreed. She always got on well with Charlie, who was nineteen years old and her brother's friend. He'd taken time out from college to come and work at Half-Moon Ranch, and said he planned to go back to his studies some time, but never did. 'Lucky gives him a signal to say hi, but he turns right around and lopes off through the trees. It's weird!'

'It sure is. He was so quiet, I thought I was seeing a ghost!' Charlie grinned.

'Me too.' Holding up her crossed fingers, she thought ahead. 'Here's hoping we get a third shot at tempting him down,' she whispered.

The snow-mover crawled up the hill, ploughing snow to one side, deeper and deeper into the arctic scene.

'Yeah, third time lucky!' Charlie agreed.

By the time they reached Elk Pass, it was nine-thirty and the snow had stopped.

It was all blue sky and white peaks, like an ad for a ski resort without the cable-cars. The untouched snow glistened. Overhead, an eagle soared.

Inside the high cab, Charlie flicked switches and pulled on the brake. The snow-mover ground to a halt on a flat stretch of track. 'We walk from here,' he told Kirstie, picking up the bag of oats as he jumped down from the cab.

She didn't need to ask why leaving the machine behind was a good idea. For a start, they needed to make their way overland towards Miners' Ridge. Secondly, by approaching Joe's territory on foot, they had a small chance of taking the lost horse by surprise. So Kirstie made sure she had a rope slung firmly across her shoulder, then picked her way down a snowy slope after the wrangler.

'You know, we ain't gonna bring him in using force,' Charlie said quietly as they approached the ridge. 'He's a whole lot stronger than us.'

Kirstie nodded, then paused for a rest. It was hard work walking through the drifts; she'd worked up some body heat and her lungs had begun to ache. At this altitude, her breath came short. 'I never use force with a horse. I reckon you gotta treat 'em nice, maybe try to be a little bit smarter than them.'

'But this horse is cute,' Charlie pointed out, scanning the ridge in vain for hoof-prints. 'He ran away and learned to live on the mountain; for a herd animal who's naturally terrified of predators, that's pretty darned smart.'

Again she agreed. 'But you can't call him wild. He's had people around him some time, some place. He learned how to wear a headcollar and follow a lead-rope. And he must know people equal food. So we use that.'

Deciding that the open stretch of hillside where they stood was as good a place as any, Kirstie took the bag of oats from Charlie. While he scooped a shallow depression in the snow, she opened the bag and scattered the oats lightly into the hole. 'No elk this time!' she pleaded, looking up at the blue sky. 'And no hungry mule deer or black bears. Just a lone Appaloosa who knows it's time to come down from the mountain!'

They retreated and waited on the lonely ridge, feeling the faint heat of the wintry sun in the thin atmosphere as it rose higher in the sky.

'Why do you reckon he ran away?' Charlie asked, arms folded, his back against a tree trunk, black stetson pulled well down to keep the glare from his eyes.

Kirstie shook her head. 'It's a mystery.'

'Hadley once told me a story about a lost horse named Hopalong. He was a big black-and-white paint; your grandpa's horse, steady as a rock. Hopalong saw your grandpa through seven years of round-ups, driving the cattle down from Bear Hunt Overlook and Eden Lake.'

As Charlie's story unfolded, Kirstie's gaze ranged over the white mountain and her mind drifted back to the time when she was a little kid and Half-Moon Ranch was still a working ranch. In those days, the family would drive out from Denver; Kirstie and Matt, her mom and dad. It was her dad who had first got her used to horses, lifting her on to the back of an easy-going grey called Sugar when Kirstie was just three years old. She still recalled those first lurching steps as Sugar walked her across the corral, her dad running alongside and telling her to hold tight to the saddle horn.

'Then, one spring, old Hopalong and your grandpa were riding up beyond the lake, looking for strays.' Charlie too was scanning the empty horizon. 'All of a sudden, from behind a heap of logs, out jumps one ugly, big, black bear who scares Hopalong half to death. The bear's up on his hind legs, his mouth's open and snarling, and for some reason he's pretty mad. Up goes Hopalong, rearing all the way back, then down he comes, bucking like crazy. And this is a horse who never said boo.'

'What happened to Grandpa?' Kirstie blocked out the picture of her dad holding her fast in the saddle. That was then. Now he lived in the city with a new wife and family. She and Matt never visited.

'He came off, broke a leg and had to crawl back to the trail until Hadley came along. Hopalong was long gone. So was the bear. But that old paint had such a scare, nothing could bring him down from Eagle's Peak for four whole weeks.'

'What did they try?'

'The same as us. A couple of guys went up, and these were prize-winning cowboys, but they couldn't get near enough to Hopalong to even throw a rope. That horse had been so scared by the bear he'd just about jumped out of his own skin and into some other horse's. He was acting like he was wild and mean and bad, yet he'd been the friendliest, most laid-back old horse on the ranch.'

Kirstie was listening hard. 'Did they get him back?'

'Hadley said in the end he came down of his own accord. But he stayed up on the mountain all spring, flitting through the trees, keeping well away from the wranglers. Course, he had plenty of good grazing at that time of year.'

'Yeah.' Kirstie sighed. That was a major difference between the two stories. Hopalong hadn't had to contend with a whiteout. She was about to prompt Charlie into telling her the ending, when she stiffened and pointed.

Navaho Joe had appeared as they talked. He

was high on the ridge; a sorry figure with snow frozen into his white mane, his thick winter coat scarcely able to hide his prominent ribs. Yet he still had that noble look, head up, ears cocked, and his walk was steady as he set off towards them. He kept them carefully in his sights as he threaded through the tall trees, scenting the food spread out for him by the human visitors.

Kirstie stood where she was, as still and quiet as could be. Hunger was driving Joe closer, his warm breath filling the air with clouds of steam, his feet crunching deep into snow drifts.

He was within twenty yards, stopping, flicking his ears towards them, watching them constantly. He came on; ten yards away now, then close enough to rope him if they wanted. But then what? He was stronger, as Charlie had said. With a rope around his neck, he would pull and surge away. The rope would burn their palms, Joe would run free.

They held their breaths and waited. The Appaloosa's eye was fixed on them as he bent his head and picked at the scattered oats.

'I'm gonna try moving in!' Kirstie whispered to Charlie. This was the closest yet she'd come to

Joe; she could see the fear in his brown eyes, the tension in his muscles. 'Don't be scared!' she murmured, approaching softly.

Her foot crunched in the snow. Up went Joe's head with a sudden jerk. The worn lead-rope snaked into the air.

'Easy!' She stopped, let him slowly settle back into feeding, then inched closer. 'No one's gonna hurt you.'

By now, she was so near to the horse that she could reach out and take hold of his headcollar. But she did nothing for a while except wait.

His head was down, his lips picking at the last of the oats. His eye and his ear said, 'I know you're there. Don't come any closer!'

'You're beautiful!' she whispered, praying that her voice would calm him. She let him finish chewing then watched him stretch out his head towards her; almost nudging her with his white nose. Her hands stayed in her pockets, offering no threat.

Joe's head swayed. His warm breath was in her face. She could see her own reflection in his glistening eye.

'Hey!' she murmured, taking one hand out of

her pocket. 'Hey, lost horse, how're you doing?'

Softly her hand touched his neck. She felt the muscles beneath the soft, damp fur quiver and flinch. Her other hand reached up to take hold of the halter.

It was a move too far. Joe twisted his head and wrenched away. The raw end of the lead-rope whipped against Kirstie's hand. She felt the pain and jerked it back.

This sudden movement spooked the horse, who now swung away and kicked out with his hind legs.

'Watch out, Kirstie!' Charlie saw the flurry of snow and the horse's back legs lashing out. He made a run to push her sideways off the ridge. Together they rolled ten or fifteen yards, and landed harmlessly in a soft drift, breathless but unhurt.

But Kirstie knew that their chance was gone. As she staggered to her feet, sinking deeper into the drift, she saw the horse rear and turn, then set off at a lope along the windswept ridge.

'Call him!' Charlie cried, still lying flat in the snow.

'It's no good; I blew it!' she whispered, following Joe's flight with helpless, hopeless eyes. 'He's gone!'

She'd failed to win his trust; and worse, she was certain that she'd condemned him to a slow death on the frozen mountain. Her heart ached for him as he loped on into the snow.

5

'Kirstie was *this* near to bringing the lost horse in!' Charlie told Matt and Hadley. The young wrangler held up his hand and made a narrow gap between his thumb and forefinger.

They stood in the yard at Half-Moon Ranch, discussing the morning's events.

'Did you try to follow him?' Matt asked, watching Kirstie cross the porch, head ducked down, obviously not wanting to join in the conversation.

Charlie shook his head. 'We only had the snow-mover, remember! It don't move above five miles an hour!'

'But leastways the horse had a good feed?' Hadley checked, turning into the barn to refill the wooden mangers with alfalfa and to check out a couple of minor problems with loose shoes.

Kirstie sighed as she kicked the snow from her boots and took off her hat. Inside the house, she found her mom working at her desk and told her the story of the near miss. 'We were *this* close!' she insisted, imitating Charlie's gesture.

'I'm real sorry, honey.' Sandy gave her a tired smile.

'If I hadn't jerked back when the rope hit my hand, I reckon we had a good chance of bringing him in.' Time and again on the slow journey back, Kirstie had replayed the exact sequence of events. Now she paced the floor of her mom's office, still unable to let it go.

'Don't you go wearing a hole in my rug!' Sandy tried to make her lighten up, but her own voice lacked its usual spark. She stood up to put an arm around Kirstie's shoulder. 'You know, no way is this your fault!'

'It feels like it is!' Why hadn't Joe felt he could

trust her? Why had he seen her as an enemy when all she wanted to do was save his life?

Squeezing her hand, Sandy pushed a stray strand of hair back from her flushed cheek. 'This afternoon I'd like you to drive into town with me. Lennie Goodman brought his snow-mover down from Lone Elm and cleared the track out to the main road while you and Charlie worked on Elk Pass. It means we can get through, no problem.'

'Why do we need to go to town?' Seeing her mom's preoccupied face as she went back to her desk, Kirstie broke free from her worries about Joe.

'I have some chores. We have to shop at Eight-til-Late, and I need to take this small ad into the *San Luis Times* office. Then Bonnie Goodman has invited us to call in at the diner.' Handing a sheet of paper to Kirstie, Sandy ran a hand through her fair hair and glanced out of the window at Matt and Charlie still talking in the yard.

Kirstie read the carefully made-out ad. 'Help Wanted' it said in bold letters. 'Experienced wrangler needed for dude ranch. Apply in writing to S. Scott, Half-Moon Ranch, Route 5, San Luis, Colorado.'

'What for? Is Charlie going back to college?' She asked the first question that flashed into her head. Her second thought focused on Hadley. 'Experienced wrangler', it said. That meant Hadley, not Charlie. 'Oh no!'

Sandy nodded slowly, without turning round. 'Hadley quit,' she said quietly. 'I can hardly believe it. Hadley! He says it's time to hang up his boots. And I just don't know how we're gonna get by without him!'

'Why?' Kirstie asked the old wrangler. She'd sought him out in the barn, found him stacking bales of hay into a barrow and wheeling them through to Moose's stall.

'A man's entitled to quit his job,' Hadley said shortly. He cut open the first hay bale with the sharp, horn-handled knife which he kept tucked into his belt.

'But this isn't just a job!' As she'd reminded him when they first talked it through, Half-Moon Ranch was Hadley's life. He had no wife, no children, nowhere to live except the bunkhouse across the yard from the corral.

'I'm sixty-five,' he said stubbornly. 'In my time

I broke just about every bone in my body; working with bovines, training up new horses. Now they fixed those bones for me at the hospital, but it don't mean they don't still ache when the wind blows in a mean direction off the Peak. And aching bones make it hard for a man to get up at four in the morning and drive a snowplough out on the trails.'

'You don't have to!' Kirstie broke in. 'Let Charlie do that.'

He shook his head then forked hay into the old grey gelding's stall. Moose stood in one corner, quietly watching. 'Your mom needs a younger head wrangler,' he insisted.

'She doesn't. She wants you to stay on!' Taking a curry comb from the ledge, Kirstie began to groom Moose with strong, firm strokes. She hoped to wear away at Hadley's resolve and make him change his mind.

But no. He worked away at the straw bedding without looking round. 'I quit,' he said, determined as ever.

'Where will you go? What will you do?' Kirstie combed a patient Moose, feeling her throat tighten and her eyes begin to fill with tears.

Hadley scattered straw. The brim of his hat covered his thin, lined face as he made the bed fresh and thick. 'I'll rent a room in town,' he muttered. 'Don't you worry none about me.'

That afternoon, Sandy and Kirstie's first call was at the *San Luis Times* office on Main Street, where they received a warm greeting from Marcie Ford, who ran small ads.

'How're y'all handling the whiteout up at Half-Moon Ranch?' she asked them in a slow, Texan drawl. Married to the newspaper's editor, Greg Ford, Marcie favoured a fancy style of dress which included a fringed suede jacket the colour of mulberries and matching nail polish. Her long, glossy hair was black as a raven's wing.

Handing over the paper containing the information about Hadley's vacant position, Sandy began to explain to Marcie why her head wrangler had quit. Meanwhile, Greg Ford himself came out of the back office carrying a heavy stack of newspapers hot off the press. He dumped them on a table and showed Kirstie the top copy.

'You seen this lead story on page 3?' he asked her.

She took the newspaper from him, opened the pages and read the big, bold headline.

'Wildflower, Come Home!'

'Yeah?' she gave Greg a puzzled glance, deliberately closing the paper up again. She'd glimpsed a black-and-white picture of a horse under the headline, her heart had given a thud and she'd chickened out from reading the rest.

'I kinda guessed you'd be interested in the story.' Greg spoke low and slow, like his wife. He was tall, lean and grey haired, and had been the editor of the *San Luis Times* for thirty years. Nothing about small town America shocked or surprised him, he told the kids at school when he paid his annual visit to give a talk on journalism. Bodies under porches, husbands killing wives, wives poisoning husbands, kids going crazy with guns and drugs; that stuff wasn't confined to the cities and never had been. It was his job to report the facts and not judge.

'Hmm.' Normally, yes; Kirstie would be the first to read a piece about a horse called 'Wildflower, Come Home!' But there was something about the picture that made her close the page.

'A nice human interest story,' Greg insisted,

taking the paper back and opening it up again. 'It has all the ingredients: two guys offering a five hundred dollar reward for the recovery of a lost horse, various sightings between here and Mineville, and now winter closing in and putting a good outcome in jeopardy.'

'You mean, the horse will freeze to death if they don't track him down fast?' Kirstie translated the last comment through gritted teeth. There was no doubt about it; this was Navaho Joe's story that Greg was describing. Wildflower? How could any sane person give a soft-sounding, romantic name like that to the explosively beautiful, strong Appie on Elk Pass? 'Did you talk to these guys?' she asked the editor as Sandy finished her business with Marcie.

'I met with them. They drove up here yesterday, before the bad snow set in, came into the office and asked, could I do a piece about their lost horse. They gave me this picture.' Greg pushed the photograph under Kirstie's nose.

She glanced down. Yes; Wildflower was Joe. The horse in the picture had the same pattern of light, freckled markings, the white mane and tail, the same proud, wild look. But for the picture he'd been stuck in front of a fake Wild West saloon, complete with porch and boardwalk, with a sign over the swing doors that read 'Buckaroos Trading Post – Live the Legend!'

'That's taken outside their place in Mineville,' Greg explained with a thin smile. 'It sells Western Wear and tack.'

Sandy came and looked over Kirstie's shoulder. 'Yeah, a nice piece of free product placement,' she grinned. 'You'd charge me two hundred dollars for that much space to advertise Half-Moon Ranch!'

'Cynic!' Greg quipped back. 'These guys care about their horse, they really do!'

'Really?' Sandy echoed, zipping up her coat, ready to leave.

Greg followed her and Kirstie on to the porch. 'I understood you saw him up on Eagle's Peak!' he called after them. 'And here I was thinking you might want to claim the five hundred dollars reward.'

No way! Kirstie marched on down the main street towards the End of Trail Diner. The wind bit into her cheeks and whipped her hair back from her face. She thought of pieces of silver and the betrayal of a free spirit. Because, however you looked at it, sending 'Wildflower' back to Buckaroos, to take part in a fake Wild West charade, was just that – a betrayal.

'. . . But leaving Joe out there to freeze will kill him for sure!' Lisa protested.

Kirstie and Sandy had walked into the diner and into the centre of the problem; for who should be sitting there eating bacon sandwiches with fried onion rings but Ed and Jerry Fraser?

'Sandy!' Bonnie Goodman had rushed out from behind her counter to introduce her to the Frasers. 'They got snowed in last night and rented a room across town at The Silver Dollar. They'll be real pleased to meet you!'

Meanwhile, Lisa had dragged Kirstie into the far corner of the room.

'Are they for real?' Kirstie ignored her friend's warning about the danger the Appie faced from the cold and glared across the rows of booths. Each booth contained a table with a red-checked cloth and high-backed bench-seats. Salt and pepper, sauce bottles and menu cards were neatly set out; the whole place looked orderly and efficient.

'What do you mean?' In spite of their earlier talks on the subject of Navaho Joe, Lisa wasn't prepared for Kirstie's reaction, nor the dark looks she was giving the visitors from Mineville.

'See what they're wearing!' Kirstie hissed scornfully, while her mom shook hands with two small, heavy guys with big, dark moustaches. One, a little balder and older than the other, was dressed in full, fancy, traditional western wear, complete with long black jacket, Mexican-style embroidered vest and bootlace tie. The younger one had gone for a more casual style of checkered shirt, red neckerchief and white stetson.

'What's wrong with it?'

'There's not a speck of dirt on them!' Kirstie hissed scornfully, contrasting them with Hadley and Charlie at the ranch. 'They never did a day's work in their lives!'

'Whatever!' Lisa shrugged and walked away with an expression that showed she wished Kirstie would hurry up and come to her senses.

By this time, Sandy was calling Kirstie over to join them, her voice cool, her gesture stiff and awkward. 'Ed, this is my daughter, Kirstie. Kirstie; Ed Fraser.'

Kirstie's slim hand was shaken by a soft, fat one with stubby fingers and a thick covering of coarse black hair. She looked into a pair of small, mud-grey eyes and a mouth that smiled meaninglessly behind the heavy moustache.

'And this is Jerry Fraser,' Sandy said to Kirstie. 'They'd like to hear your story about the sightings of their horse on Eagle's Peak.'

Kirstie cleared her throat. 'I couldn't say for sure that it was *your* horse.'

'Who else could it belong to?' A frown replaced the shallow smile behind Ed Fraser's moustache. 'It's a brown-and-white Appie, ain't it?'

'Y-yeah . . .'

'Wearing a halter and a lead-rope?'

'Yeah . . .'

'So, it's Wildflower.' Ed slapped his palm against the table, then shoved his plate away with the heel of his hand. 'We bought him in the spring as a mascot horse for Buckaroos. The plan is for Jerry here to ride Wildflower up and down Main Street all kitted out in fancy cowboy gear, attracting business to our store; a kind of walking advertisement, get it?'

Kirstie stared at him without expression and nodded slowly. 'Who wears the fancy gear; you or the horse?' she asked Jerry.

'Huh? Oh yeah, I get it!' He laughed loudly, then took a loud gulp of coffee. 'Well, I wear the shirts and the boots and the vests, and the horse wears the saddles and bridles. So I guess we both look pretty fancy!'

And pretty stupid! Kirstie thought, her eyelids flickering. She was angry on Joe's behalf. How could they treat him like a freak in a sideshow for tourists to stare at? Before long, they'd be offering rides down the busy Main Street at fifty cents per person. 'How come he ran away?' she asked.

'Who said he ran?' Ed Fraser prickled at the question. He looked at her through narrowed eyes.

'He broke his lead-rope,' she pointed out, unwavering in her return stare.

'Yeah, that was down to some fool driver in a Jeep,' Jerry Fraser explained. 'Our Main Street in Mineville is pretty gridlocked with traffic most days. We get plenty of visitors for the steam train and they spend money in our store, so I ain't complaining. The train track runs across the street, so six times per day the gates come down to stop the traffic. This one day I'm leading Wildflower down Main Street. We have to wait at the gate for the train to pass through. I tie him to a post and I'm ten yards up the street, talking with my friend.'

'Didn't the noise of the train scare him?' Lisa cut in.

'He's pretty much gotten used to it,' Jerry told her. 'Sure, he's a little edgy, but it's no problem until the day I'm talking about. There's a guy in a Jeep down the street some. He doesn't understand why the cars are waiting in line, so he jams his fist on the horn. This makes Wildflower jump in the air, and just then the train comes by, so he jumps some more.'

Kirstie pictured the frightened animal straining at the rope as jarring noises filled his ears and the train rolled by snorting out steam.

Ed Fraser seemed irritated by his younger brother's long-winded account. He broke in to finish the story. 'The horse jerks so hard on the rope he snaps it in two and runs off down the street, trailing the busted part after him. A whole heap of guys try to catch on to him, but he's so spooked he rears up at each and every one and makes a clean getaway. Next thing we know is, he's clear out of town, across the South Fork River and heading for the hills.'

'That was early September,' Jerry said.

'And did you go after him?' Kirstie could understand now why Joe had turned so mistrustful and wild. Any horse would after that experience. A giant iron train belching out steam must be twenty times worse than a black bear or a mountain lion.

'Sure.' Ed cast more wary glances in her direction. 'But we got a business to run. We can't spend twenty-four hours per day looking for some damn fool runaway horse!'

'But now the tourist season's over and we got more time,' the milder Jerry continued. 'We picked up the trail about a week ago when we heard of an Appie roaming free west of San Luis. So we made a few phone calls and narrowed it down, making sure this was Wildflower. A couple of days back we spoke to a truck driver who uses Route 5 pretty much every day. He told us about the notice in Bonnie's diner, and that's how come we're here.'

'So!' Sandy took a deep breath and looked anxiously at Kirstie. 'Ed and Jerry got snowed in last night, but now their luck's turned. You show up while they're eating and, hey, you're the very person who can tell them exactly where Wildflower is hanging out!'

She stared back at her mom with wide, pleading eyes. *Don't make me do this*!

'Kirstie!' Sandy said in a firm voice and with a look that said, *The horse belongs to them. There's not a thing we can do*!

'So?' Ed Fraser demanded. 'You pinpoint the place and first thing tomorrow we drive out there and bring him in.'

Kirstie swallowed hard and thought about lying through her teeth. But her mom's clear grey eyes were fixed on her. 'He's up on Eagle's Peak,' she muttered.

'We already know that,' Ed Fraser pressed, pulling a map from his coat pocket and spreading it on the checkered tablecloth. 'It's a big mountain. We were hoping for a little more help.'

'Near Miners' Ridge.' Kirstie saw her mom point out the ridge on the map; a series of thin

73

contour lines north of Dead Man's Canyon, crowding closer and closer together. She sighed and hung her head as Sandy's finger traced the directions she gave. 'Two hundred yards up the mountain from there on Elk Pass. That's where Joe . . . I mean, Wildflower, is hanging out!'

6

'That horse is finding shelter up there for sure!' Ed Fraser admitted he was no expert on weather conditions on Eagle's Peak, but even to an outsider like him, it was obvious that the Appaloosa couldn't have survived without help.

It was late Friday afternoon. The Fraser brothers had spent two days searching the area without success. Now they were down at Half-Moon Ranch planning their next move.

'That ain't possible!' was Hadley's reaction to Ed's remark. He'd heard the silver pick-up pull up in the yard and had come out of the barn with Kirstie and Charlie to learn how their search was progressing. 'If he'd been hanging round any of the ranches like the Lazy B or Ponderosa Pines, we'd have heard for sure.'

'Are you certain he's still there?' Sandy asked. She'd left off discussions with her two builders and walked down from Brown Bear Cabin when she'd first seen the Frasers' truck crawling along the track between high banks of snow. With her collar up and her blue baseball cap pulled low over her forehead, her pale face was showing the stress of recent problems.

Jerry Fraser nodded curtly. 'We picked up his track a couple of times, and late yesterday afternoon we even caught sight of him by the side of a frozen stretch of water beyond Crystal Creek.'

'Eden Lake,' Kirstie's mom confirmed.

'We didn't even come close to roping him in,' Ed went on, fixing his suspicious, muddy grey stare on Kirstie. 'He still puts on a fair burst of speed, which takes me back to what I said before; I reckon he's found shelter and food.'

She felt her face turn red, despite the biting

cold. It was obvious that Ed Fraser suspected her of having his beautiful Appie secretly tucked away in the barn at nights, feasting on their best alfalfa.

'We took him some oats on Wednesday.' Charlie recalled their last contact with the lost horse. 'We were close to bringing him in, but he's been up there by himself so long he's got pretty hard to handle.'

Kirstie remembered the feel of Joe's warm breath on her hand, the look of deep mistrust in his liquid brown eye.

'If you want to know, Kirstie risked a heck of a lot to get near, and if anyone could bring your horse home, she could.' The young ranch hand had read Ed Fraser's suspicious gaze and decided to defend his boss's daughter.

'So, tell me what's happening here!' After two days of fruitless searching, the older brother's patience had worn thin. 'If you ain't helping Wildflower to make it through these sub-zero nights, who is?'

His question met a wall of silence. Charlie shrugged and turned away, Hadley returned his angry gaze with a stony look, while Sandy and Kirstie looked at each other with concern.

'You're telling me this horse is doing it himself?' Ed's normally deep voice rose a couple of octaves. He swept his arm towards the spectacular horizon. The mountains glittered pure white under a pale blue sky. 'Man, I just don't believe it!'

'Mr Fraser,' Sandy began, taking a step forward to try to calm him. 'Can I make a suggestion?'

'Go ahead.'

'Tomorrow's Saturday, right? If you drive out from San Luis early and call here on your way up to Eagle's Peak, I can promise you three or four riders to help find your horse and bring him down.' She spoke slowly and softly, ignoring Kirstie's sudden movement and little cry of protest behind her back. 'My son, Matt, will be home from college. He can show you some places on the mountain you might not have checked. And Hadley and Charlie will go along too.'

'That's good of you, ma'am.' Jerry Fraser found his manners first, and gave his brother a dig with his elbow. 'Ain't it, Ed? It's mighty considerate.'

Sandy gave a slight nod in his direction. 'That's OK. I agree with your brother; it almost defies belief that the horse can live through these conditions. And, what's worse, there's more snow forecast.'

'For Monday,' Ed Fraser grunted. 'They predict a thaw for Sunday, then twelve inches plus.'

'So no time to lose.' Sandy was brisk, ushering Kirstie across the yard towards the house, their feet crunching across the crisp, trodden surface, the heels of their boots sinking down. 'We'll see you tomorrow morning, gentlemen; bright and early!'

Charlie and Kirstie brushed the horses until they gleamed. Rodeo Rocky's brown coat caught the sun with its peculiar metallic tint; his black mane and tail were combed straight and neat. Across his broad back went the saddle, polished and softened by wear, then his shiny bit and bridle. The ex-rodeo horse's head was up, there was an air of expectancy about him as he sidled up to Lucky.

'Hey, Rocky!' Kirstie nudged him away. 'Let me tighten this cinch.' She leaned against her palomino for a better grip then pulled the strap a couple of holes tighter. Lucky danced a few steps and raised his head. He too could sense adventure in the cold, clear air.

'Seven-thirty!' Having taken the decision to stay home, Sandy stood in the corral amidst the bustle of activity. She looked at her watch and glanced up the track to the ranch gates. There was still no sign of the Frasers.

'Give them fifteen minutes, then we set off without them,' Matt decided. He was already up on Cadillac, his big white gelding, his black stetson jammed down firmly, his handsome face glum. Being volunteered by his mom for a search party to find the lost horse wasn't his idea of a weekend break from college work. 'Lachelle's planning to call at midday,' he told Sandy. 'I want to bring this Appie in and forget the whole problem by then.'

'Don't we all?' Standing nearby, Sandy reached out to hold Moose's head while Hadley mounted. The old grey quarter horse waited until his rider was settled, then ambled over to Rocky and Lucky.

'Here they come!' Kirstie was the first to spot the silver pick-up with the bright red Buckaroo logo. It stopped under the arch of rustic logs that supported the Half-Moon Ranch sign, straddling the cattle grid that kept the ranch horses on the right side of the fence. Then the passenger door swung open and a figure Kirstie hadn't been expecting sprang out.

'Hey, Kirstie!' Lisa waved both arms and began the slippery descent down the hill towards the sheltered corral. Dressed in double layers of clothes, with a thick scarf around her neck and a stetson covering her short, auburn hair, there was hardly an inch of flesh exposed.

Kirstie turned Lucky and put him into a trot across the corral. 'How come?' she quizzed as her friend slid the final few yards to level ground. Meaning: what was Lisa doing here?

'Easy. I hitched a lift.' She brushed snow from her trousers and grinned up at Kirstie.

'I can see that, crazy girl. I mean, how come you decided to help?' Kirstie hadn't called the diner, hadn't told anyone how she planned to spend her weekend.

She'd argued with her mom about it the evening before, going over the same old ground: the Frasers didn't deserve to get Navaho Joe back, they didn't have any sense of the horse's dignity and free spirit, it wasn't fair to treat him like a sideshow at a fair.

'So, do what?' Sandy had replied. 'Nothing? Let him freeze?' That was why she'd offered the help: to save Joe's life. And in the end, Kirstie had agreed it was the only way. But she didn't like it. And she hadn't slept much. She certainly hadn't confided in her best friend.

'Charlie, fix up a horse for Lisa!' Sandy yelled when she saw her well-wrapped figure scramble down the snowy slope. 'Saddle Crazy Horse. It looks like we got ourselves an extra hand!'

'So?' Kirstie grinned back at Lisa in spite of herself. 'How come?'

'The Frasers were in the diner last night,' she confessed. 'I overheard the plan and decided to show up ... surprise!' Lisa spread her hands, palms upwards. 'No way was I gonna miss the drama!'

So there were five riders – Charlie, Hadley, Matt, Kirstie and Lisa – setting off along Five Mile Creek Trail ahead of the silver pick-up. It wasn't yet eight o'clock on a fine Saturday morning, and the group hid a bunch of mixed feelings beneath their layers of warm clothes.

Matt on Cadillac wanted to get the whole thing

over and be back by lunch to speak to his girlfriend. He only half-listened to Charlie's jokey stories as he rode alongside on Rocky. Charlie didn't seem to care. He fooled around, dumping snow from overhanging branches on to Matt's head as his friend wove after him through the pine trees in Dead Man's Canyon. Then he led him down a culvert that came to a dead end and pelted him with snowballs.

Hadley watched the young men's raucous games without reacting. He kept Moose on a steady course, refused to waste energy even on talking, and kept to himself his thoughts about their chances of succeeding in what they'd set out to do.

Maybe he was dwelling on his own recent decision to quit; a good move or a bad move? Too late to change his mind? Maybe not? He rode silently, third in line after Matt and Charlie, eyes on the upper slopes beyond Miners' Ridge, alert to every movement.

Then came Kirstie and Lisa, talking quietly. The even gait of the horses as they took the snow-covered slopes in their stride settled the friends into sharing how they felt about Navaho Joe. Lisa said yes, she could understand how Kirstie didn't want him to be a Buckaroos mascot horse for the rest of his life. 'It *is* kind of humiliating,' she admitted.

Kirstie explained how much she pitied and admired the lost horse. 'It's like he's a hero . . . like freedom means everything to him.' She tried to explain Joe's special strength. She'd only seen him twice in her life, yet he was etched in her memory. He appeared there, pale and beautiful, shadowy and silent, always alone, always running.

As the girls talked in low, serious voices, they could hear the chug of the silver pick-up close behind them. The Frasers had declined Sandy's offer of horses for them to ride, had said they preferred to drive the vehicle as far up the mountain as Elk Pass, and from there they would go on foot if necessary.

'I guess they don't ride much back in Mineville,' Lisa whispered, as the line of horses cut off along Miners' Ridge and the pick-up kept to the ploughed track.

Matt had fixed up a meeting-point about a half mile up the road. The two brothers were to wait for the riders if they arrived at the landmark rock before them; the boulder where Navaho Joe had first appeared to Kirstie during the round-up of Jim Mullins' cows.

The land beyond Miners' Ridge was wild and rocky, with fewer trees and long, steep slopes of unbroken snow. Glancing to left and right, then back towards the narrow valleys, Kirstie was reminded that there was an awful lot of mountain where the fugitive horse might hide.

But one idea that Ed Fraser had voiced the evening before stuck with her and kept resurfacing now. The Appie's owner had been convinced that the runaway had found shelter on the mountain, though Hadley, who ought to know best, said there was nowhere this side of the mountain and only Coyote Cow Station to the east.

The cow station? Kirstie didn't even know exactly where it was or who it belonged to. But it definitely sounded like shelter. Maybe Joe had found his way there. She was about to share her theory with Lisa, when a shout from Charlie up ahead made them urge Lucky and Crazy Horse on.

'Lost horse!' the young wrangler yelled. He was

up on Elk Pass, beside a stack of felled pine trunks, pointing down into the next valley, his cry loud enough to alert not only the girls, but also the Frasers who were still trundling up the track. The pick-up roared and gathered speed, its tyres sliding sideways on a bend, churning up ice and struggling to make it to the stack of timber.

'Down by Coyote Lake!' Charlie's voice was high with tension as Kirstie and Lisa drew level. He pointed half a mile across a windswept, open slope to a small, frozen lake on an unprotected plateau.

Kirstie shaded her eyes against the brilliant glare of the hillside and picked out the iced-over water, which ran two hundred yards in length, but only about twenty across. There were three lonely lodgepole pines on the near shore, and under the middle tree an animal standing still and silent, its pale coat acting as camouflage against the snow.

'Yep,' Hadley said, to confirm the sighting. He set Moose off at a determined, steady walk, heading diagonally across the unmarked slope.

Kirstie's heart missed a beat. How lonely Joe

looked; how small and how lost.

'We need skis for this baby,' Matt muttered, clicking his tongue at Cadillac to follow Moose. As he disappeared from the top of the slope, he yelled a loud message for Ed and Jerry Fraser to come after them on foot. Then he ordered Lisa and Crazy Horse to split off to the right, Kirstie and Lucky to the left in a pincer movement that was intended to cut off the runaway horse's line of retreat in both directions. 'Me, Charlie and Hadley will head straight for him. There's the lake behind him, so this way we got him pretty well cornered under those trees.'

As the riders fanned out and the two men on foot backed them up, the lonely horse by the lake watched them approach. Kirstie's gaze was fixed on him, trusting Lucky to pick his own way. Why didn't Joe make a break for it? she wondered. Was he too weak by this time to run?

His pursuers drew within two hundred yards, then one hundred. She could see now that he sure was in a bad way; thinner than before, with an open cut across one knee as if he'd stumbled and fallen on sharp rock. His white mane was whipped by the wind into twisted, matted locks; the muscle on his shoulders and neck had begun to waste so that he looked pitifully thin. Still he held his head up, defying them to come any closer.

'Easy, boy!' Hadley pulled Moose up some thirty yards from where the Appaloosa had taken shelter under the tree. Matt and Charlie spread out behind him, as by this time Kirstie and Lisa had reached their respective ends of the small lake. As Hadley had predicted, they had the horse well and truly trapped.

Kirstie pulled Lucky up on the frozen shore. She shook her head; *Poor Joe!*

The weakened, exhausted horse seemed to be waiting for their next move. He looked undecided. Then he must have spotted Ed and Jerry Fraser stumbling along on foot, because it was when Ed yelled an order at Hadley to ride right in and get a rope around Wildflower's neck that he made his choice. He turned his head towards Lisa, then towards Kirstie. He took two steps forward, but quickly veered round and ran back the way he'd come.

'No!' Kirstie shouted. That way was the snowy

shore and the ice-covered lake. She set Lucky into a lope towards him. 'Come back!'

The Appie ignored her. His hooves crunched over uneven snow and then stepped out on to the smooth ice.

Hadley put up his hand to warn everyone to hold it. Kirstie reined Lucky back. The palomino churned up snow and skidded to a halt. They all froze in the saddle and prayed.

'Stop!' Kirstie whispered to herself.

The lost horse trod across the frozen lake. His step was hollow, his footing uncertain on the slippery white surface. The ice cracked and splintered, but he walked on.

'Please!' Kirstie begged.

The sound of splintering ice seemed magnified inside her head; a crack loud as a branch breaking from a tree in a storm. Then a lethal zigzag appeared on the surface, opening up, allowing water to ooze through.

As if in a dream, Kirstie clicked at Lucky and urged him on.

'Hold it!' Suddenly someone had loped towards her and seized Lucky's rein. It was Matt, stopping her from following Joe, holding her back, telling her she was crazy. 'Don't even think about it!' he warned.

So she had to stand by and watch the crack widen. The snap of breaking ice pierced her brain. Clear water gushed up from the depths, washed around Joe's feet and legs. He plunged on towards the centre, surrounded by breaking ice, his hooves striking through the brittle layer, further and further from safety.

Kirstie gasped as finally the ice gave way.

Joe sank into the dark water. It closed over his pale head and he vanished from sight.

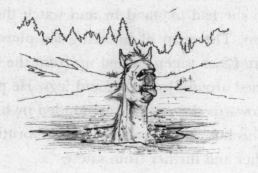

7

'Amazing!' Matt shook his head then stared across the lake.

'I've never seen a horse do that before!' Charlie hauled in the rope that he'd thrown to rescue Joe when his head had bobbed back up to the surface. The lasso had fallen short and the horse had swum out of reach.

'He bulldozed right through that ice to the far shore!' Lisa gasped, watching him now as he clambered to safety. 'Thank goodness the winter freeze hasn't taken hold already; then the ice would've been way too thick for him to have made it.'

As it was, Joe had resurfaced and forced his way through the thin ice to the far shore, swimming strongly, without a single glance back at his pursuers.

Kirstie breathed again. Joe had survived the seemingly suicidal plunge into the icy water with only one idea in his head: freedom!

'You OK?' Lisa asked her, reining Crazy Horse close alongside Lucky. 'You look like you're in shock.'

Kirstie's hands trembled, her stomach fluttered, her teeth were clenched tight. 'I'm fine!' she shuddered, unable to drag her gaze away from the fleeing horse.

Navaho Joe had reached firm ground. A bedraggled, dripping spectacle, he was forcing himself on after his ordeal, staggering up the steep slope across snow that had been criss-crossed by small, light animals such as foxes or coyotes. Their tiny, neat paw-prints tracked down to the water's edge and up again, disappearing into the trees along a ridge some half a mile from where the group of riders stood.

'So?' Ed Fraser demanded, struggling knee-deep through the snow up to Hadley. 'What are we waiting for?'

Moose backed off, sank to his haunches in a drift, then pulled himself clear. Hadley sat patiently until his horse was steady again. 'Do we try some more?' he asked Matt, glancing up at the sun gathering strength in the cloudless blue sky.

'Sure we do!' Ed cried furiously. He could see his valuable Appie disappearing fast into a bunch of pine trees.

Matt did his best to ignore him. 'What're you thinking?' he asked the old ranch hand.

'I'm thinking avalanche,' Hadley replied, matter-of-fact as ever.

But Lisa turned to Kirstie in a panic. 'Avalanche!' She mouthed the words, her green eyes wide with alarm.

Still watching Joe, Kirstie nodded. Hot sun on top of recent snow meant that the drifts in the deep ravines would begin to melt and slide. Cracks would appear on the smooth white surface of the upper slopes. If the temperatures held up, huge sections would become unstable. Some

94

would shift, break away and come crashing down into the valleys.

'Pray for bad weather!' she whispered to her friend with a wry grin, as Matt turned to the Fraser brothers and tried to explain that staying out on Eagle's Peak in these conditions could prove dangerous.

'You're saying we give up?' Ed Fraser retorted, unwilling as ever to take advice. He saw his runaway horse reach the cover of the trees as he stood locked in time-wasting argument with Matt.

'Maybe we should do as they say.' Jerry was worried as his gaze scanned the glistening horizon for telltale cracks in the snow.

'No way!' Ed turned on his brother with open contempt. 'These guys can do what they want, but we're heading right back to the pick-up and driving on through the pass.'

Kirstie frowned, still longing for another glimpse of Joe as he vanished into the trees, feeling a fresh alarm creep through her body. The horse was amazing, as Matt said. He'd survived for more than eight weeks, foraging and fighting off enemies. Somehow he'd made it through days of freezing cold and he'd shrugged off all attempts to recapture him. But in these freak weather conditions his free spirit might now prove fatal. Even Navaho Joe couldn't survive an avalanche – that much she knew.

'I don't think you should do that, sir!' Charlie tried to remonstrate with Ed Fraser, who was heading back to the track where the silver pick-up was parked.

But frustration drove the shop owner on. He reached the truck and wrenched open the door, waiting impatiently for Jerry to join him. 'We'll take a look over the far side of the pass!' he yelled back at the watching group. 'With luck, the horse will head that way too.'

'Crazy man!' Matt muttered. He was preparing to call Sandy back at the ranch on his two-way radio to bring her up to date. Listening to her reply, he discovered that Hadley had guessed right; there was an avalanche warning out from the weather station. Weekend skiers had been advised to stay off the slopes. Sandy herself told Matt to bring his group back to the ranch double-quick.

Charlie gave up the argument and rode Rodeo Rocky to join them. 'What can we do to stop them?' he asked Hadley.

'Nothin'.' The old wrangler shook his head. 'They ain't breaking no law.'

'Huh.' Lisa spoke for them all as Ed Fraser started the pick-up engine and began to drive the vehicle up the hill at a snail's pace. Ahead lay a series of hairpin bends, vanishing round the side of the mountain. 'Maybe not; but they're risking their necks and they sure as heck ain't gonna risk mine!'

Everyone was agreed; Ed and Jerry Fraser had placed themselves in grave danger.

'The problem is, this type of weather don't look bad,' Charlie was saying to Lisa, while Kirstie took the radio from Matt and tried to keep in touch with what was going on back at the ranch. The four, plus Hadley, had all set off across country, along Miners' Ridge and into Dead Man's Canyon, backtracking the way they'd come.

'Sure,' Lisa agreed. 'The blue sky makes it kinda pretty. But it takes a fool to ignore Hadley's advice and go on up the mountain.'

'Let's hope the old guy's wrong for once!' Charlie tried to lighten the mood, speaking loud enough for Hadley to overhear. The head wrangler ducked his head but said nothing.

Meanwhile, Kirstie picked up crackly messages on the radio.

'Lazy B to Half-Moon Ranch. Are you receiving?'

'Half-Moon Ranch, Sandy here. Go ahead, Jim.'

'Did you pick up the avalanche warning out your way? Over.'

'We sure did. Weather station predicts temperatures way above freezing. Over.'

'Smiley's up in the Forest Guard chopper, keeping an eye on things. So far, so good. Over.'

'Good to hear that, Jim. But avalanche is the last thing we need. Listen, if Smiley sees anything and calls you, will you call back and tell me? Over.'

'Sure thing, Sandy . . .'

Jim Mullins' voice faded in a static mush as Kirstie and her group descended into the canyon. Here, in the sunless, narrow ravine, the horses went in single file, finding the going tough and blowing out clouds of steam into the suddenly cold air.

For half an hour, as they wound down through the trees and until they got a clear view of Five

Mile Creek in the valley below, Kirstie switched off the radio. When she turned it on again, she tuned in on a rapid exchange between Jim Mullins and a voice she recognised as belonging to Smiley Gilpin, the Forest Guard.

'. . . Vehicle overturned on Elk Pass! Over.' Smiley reported, against the loud drone of a helicopter's blades.

'. . . Exact location? Over.' Jim's reply was immediate.

'East of the Peak, by Coyote Cow Station. Silver pick-up, turned on its back, no sign of occupants! Over.' Smiley's voice crackled and hissed on the radio.

By this time, Lisa had latched on to the message. 'They smashed the pick-up!' she yelled ahead at Matt and Charlie. Behind the girls, Hadley made up ground so that he too could listen in.

'I'll send some guys out from Lazy B!' Jim told Smiley. 'They'll get there quicker than the rescue team from San Luis. Over.'

'Just hold on!' Smiley's voice was drowned out by the chopper, then came back through. 'I've been down close as I can. There definitely ain't no driver in there. You got any idea who it might be? Over.'

'Smiley, it's me, Kirstie Scott!' She broke in quickly with the information he wanted, telling the Forest Guard about the Frasers' fanatical quest to find their lost horse. Then, when Matt signalled to her that he'd like to speak to Smiley, she handed over the radio.

'We're on our way back up there,' Matt said quickly. 'We're closer than Jim's guys. Tell the San Luis rescue team that we'll do what we can until they reach the scene of the accident. Over.'

'I'm heading down the mountain to guide the rescue team back up,' Smiley informed them. 'You take care! Stick to the road and if it looks like any of the drifts are melting and shifting, you turn right around and go home, OK?'

Matt glanced quickly at the others. 'Sure,' he promised. He signed off and turned Cadillac back towards the ridge, muttering about damn fool city slickers who got themselves into deep trouble by ignoring good advice. 'But we gotta stick together and go and dig them out all the same,' he said.

'Sure. We can't leave them to freeze to death,' Charlie agreed, urging Rodeo Rocky out of the canyon into bright sunlight once more.

'Some of us could!' Lisa grunted resentfully. Crazy Horse was more willing than his rider to turn away from the warmth and safety of Half-Moon Ranch and head after Charlie.

Kirstie shrugged. She sympathised with her friend but, 'No, really!' she murmured, picturing the silver pick-up turned on its back, black wheels spinning, the cab embedded deep in a snow drift. Loathe Ed and Jerry Fraser as she did, they were human beings in need of help. She clicked her tongue at Lucky and nudged him on. 'Face it; we don't have a choice!'

There were two shovels near the back of the Frasers' pick-up which must have fallen out as the vehicle hit a patch of ice and turned over. Matt and Charlie each grabbed one and started to dig into the drift.

'Jeez!' Lisa shook her head at the sight that greeted them high on Elk Pass.

The truck had spun off the road and turned turtle, skidding on its roof for twenty yards down a slope until it hit a ten foot wall of snow, burying its hood deep. Both doors of the cab seemed to have burst open on impact and were now wedged into the drift. But like Smiley had said, neither Ed nor Jerry Fraser seemed anywhere to be seen.

As Matt and Charlie dug a channel towards the driver's seat to make sure that Ed Fraser hadn't been thrown clear then buried in the drift, Kirstie slid from Lucky's saddle, handed the reins to Lisa and scrambled down the slope for a closer look.

'Smell that gas!' she muttered. Approaching from the passenger side, she could see a shallow pool of fuel which had leaked through the floor of the cab. The key was in the ignition and a small red light showed that it was still switched on. Quickly she scooped snow out of the cab with her gloved hands, then reached forward to take the key out. Now at least there was no chance of a spark igniting the spilt fuel.

But as she leaned forward, she'd put her hand on a second pool of something wet which slowly seeped through her leather glove. Not gas this time; the stain was dark and sticky. Kirstie gasped as she slipped her hand clear of the glove and stared at her bright red fingertips.

'Oh, Jeez!' Lisa groaned as Kirstie held up her hand. 'Blood!'

'Which means either Ed or Jerry got hurt!' Frantically Kirstie wiped her hand in the snow. Now that she looked more closely, she could see spots of blood outside the cab, leading back up to the road. She climbed the slope to join Lisa and Hadley and wait for Matt and Charlie, who had stopped digging and come to see the thin red trail for themselves.

'At least one of them's alive!' Charlie said, breathing heavily after his spell of digging.

'*Was* alive!' Matt corrected. 'It looks like he was bleeding pretty bad.'

'The track cuts across the road and then on up.' Hadley pointed out the place where the trail of blood came to a stop.

'What the . . . ?' Matt gave an exasperated sigh as he realised what this meant. The injured Fraser brother had set off in the wrong direction to find help. 'These guys don't know the first thing about this territory,' he moaned.

Kirstie thought hard. 'Or else, he was confused after the crash.'

'Maybe he took a knock on the head, so he staggered off without any sense of where he was headed!' Lisa agreed with Kirstie's theory. 'And the other brother's still lying unconscious in that drift!' She pointed towards the upturned truck. 'You know what that means? One's in danger of bleeding to death, while the other dies of suffocation!'

'OK, I'll ride with Kirstie and Lisa along the track.' Hadley took an instant decision. 'Matt, can you and Charlie carry on digging?'

Agreeing on the plan to split up, Matt and Charlie went back to the drift while Hadley took charge of the two-way radio and led the way deeper still into Elk Pass. An occasional spot of blood told them they were on the right trail. Then, as they were about to round a bend that would take them out of sight of the wrecked truck, Kirstie heard a shout from Matt.

'We found Ed!' he yelled, cupping his hands around his mouth.

She turned Lucky and called back. 'How is he?'

'In bad shape. Unconscious but still breathing!' The faint voice drifted back up the mountain. 'Charlie's digging him out from under the truck!'

'We'll call Smiley on the radio!' An emergency message to the Forest Guard would bring him speeding over the pass in his chopper. Then Matt, Charlie and Smiley would be able to stretcher Ed Fraser off to the Emergency Room in the hospital at Renegade. Meanwhile, Kirstie, Lisa and Hadley would have to concentrate on their search for Jerry.

'That means we're on our own,' Lisa murmured, gazing up at the looming white peak, looking scared and small.

'Only until the San Luis rescue guys get here,' Kirstie reminded her, glad that Hadley was with them.

As she spoke, the old wrangler had started

sending updates to Smiley, then to Sandy Scott. He reassured Kirstie's mom that he would take good care of the girls and send them home as soon as he could. 'Don't you worry none,' he told her. 'Jerry Fraser can't get far on foot. We'll have everyone out of here by noon. Over.'

He turned off the radio and slipped it into his jacket pocket. As they began guiding their horses carefully around the icy bend and seeing new slopes of pure white snow ahead, they all picked up the muffled sound of helicopter blades.

Kirstie saw Lucky's ears flick this way and that at the unfamiliar noise. The palomino tensed up and went forward less willingly than before.

Then the Forest Guard's copter appeared over a ridge followed by the San Luis rescue team, engines throbbing, blades whirring like two monstrous dragonflies in the blue sky.

Behind Kirstie and Lucky, Crazy Horse skittered off the track, close up against a bank of snow. Hadley reined Moose to the right to pull them clear. 'Hold them steady!' he called above the churning blades. The choppers tilted, then hovered on the ridge while Smiley worked out the lie of the land and spotted the upturned pick-up. Then they surged forward, over the heads of the three waiting riders. Soon they were swooping in unison down the pass.

'OK!' Hadley gave the signal to go on.

'C'mon, Kirstie!' Lisa's face showed that she wanted to get this search over with. '. . . Kirstie!'

But Kirstie wasn't listening. She was staring at the high ridge, her head back, her mouth half open. Her heart was racing as she searched for a second glimpse of what she had just seen.

'This way!' Hadley was showing Lisa a new trickle of blood on the snow, picking up the injured man's trail once more.

But still Kirstie stared on. And there he was again, standing on the ridge clear as anything, watching them from a safe distance, more mysterious, more unreal than ever: Navaho Joe.

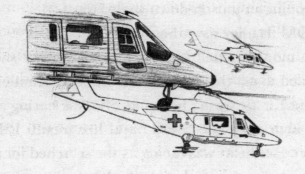

8

They found Jerry Fraser slumped against a rough palisade of pine stakes at the entrance to Coyote Cow Station. The injured man must have staggered more than a mile in the wrong direction before he'd collapsed in a snow drift close to the only shelter as far as the eye could see.

'He nearly made it inside, but not quite,' Hadley muttered, dismounting from Moose to wipe the dusting of snow from Jerry's face. His eyes were closed, his dark moustache clogged with ice.

For a moment Kirstie thought that Jerry must be dead. His lined face was almost as pale as the snow, his body huddled in an awkward position, head lolling to one side. And there was blood seeping through his thick, green-checkered woollen coat; a deep crimson stain on the white ground.

Hadley bent down close and listened to the man's chest. 'Still breathing!'

So Lisa and Kirstie clicked into action. They slid from the saddle and tied Crazy Horse and Lucky to the rough fence. Following Hadley's calm instructions, they lifted Jerry and carried him out of the wind, under the huge corrugated tin roof of the primitive barn construction.

The hundred foot long building was built of tall wooden poles and open on three sides. Inside, it consisted of rows of metal stalls which the cowboys would use to brand and process cattle. Left empty for ninety per cent of the year, in winter the cow station was exposed to the elements, perhaps providing rough, temporary shelter for the small herds of elk who remained this high up the mountain when the first snows came.

Even now, as Hadley, Lisa and Kirstie carried the unconscious man towards a warm corner, they could smell an animal presence. There was a sweet, musty stench from the trampled straw, a trail of hay across the dirt floor from old bales left behind some weeks earlier by wranglers who had worked the station.

'Easy now!' Hadley grunted, nodding towards a stall stacked with bales of decent-looking straw. 'We'll lay him on these, keep him warm, try and stop the bleeding.'

Jerry Fraser had proved a heavy, dead weight, and Kirstie's arms ached. She hung on to his legs for the final few yards, then took a deep breath as they laid him gently on the straw. Watching Hadley take off his own jacket, she rapidly started to unbutton Jerry's coat, gasping as she saw the ripped shirt and wound beneath.

By this time, Hadley was down to his T-shirt, quickly ripping his outer shirt into wide strips. He formed one into a thick pad and stepped forward to press it against Jerry's ribs. Blood from the wound oozed through, so he replaced the soaked pad with a fresh one, telling Kirstie and Lisa to throw his jacket over the lower part of

Jerry's body. 'He's gonna die of the cold if the bleeding doesn't do it first,' he muttered, pressing hard on the wound.

Kirstie saw Jerry's eyelids flicker and she heard a low moan. 'He's coming round!' she warned.

'OK, the blood flow's easing up.' Hadley decided it was time to strap the pad against the wound with longer strips of shirt. 'I reckon he's broken a couple of ribs at least. And if a rib punctures the lung, we've got big problems!'

'Give me the radio!' Lisa said, thinking quickly now that the first shock was past.

Kirstie slid her hand into. Hadley's jacket pocket and pulled the small black machine out. 'You need to run outside to pick up a signal!'

So while Lisa went off to call the rescue team for help, Kirstie and Hadley bound Jerry's chest. 'He did make it this far, remember!' Kirstie was determined not to think the worst. 'And he's a strong-looking guy!'

Hadley nodded without looking up. Minus coat and shirt in this sub-zero temperature, the old ranch hand's own body looked surprisingly fragile. The brim of his hat hid his face as he stooped to listen to Jerry's breathing, then put his blunt fingertips against the injured man's wrist to feel the pulse. 'We need more warm stuff!' he told her.

Quickly Kirstie unzipped her own padded jacket and laid it across Jerry's chest. Way down the length of the barn, she could see Lisa talking urgently into the radio. Beyond that, the wild mountainside sparkled in the sun.

Her attention was drawn back to their first-aid task by a rasping, choking noise in Jerry's throat. Hadley loosened the top button of his shirt and watched intently. The man coughed, opened his eyes and gave a low groan.

'It's OK, Mr Fraser; you had an accident but we're taking care of you!' Kirstie responded to his bewildered gaze. His eyes flicked from her to Hadley and back again, but he made no attempt to move. 'We're radioing for help right this second. You just gotta hold on until the chopper gets here!'

'They're on their way!' Lisa ran back into the barn. 'Smiley has stretchered Ed Fraser down the mountain in the Forest Guard chopper. The Rescue Team is headed up this way!'

Already they could hear the low drone of the helicopter approaching.

'OK, we're not gonna move you before those guys arrive,' Hadley told Jerry. 'There's space for them to land by the palisade, so we won't have to winch you up. From now on, we leave it to the experts!'

Fraser groaned and nodded. He still looked like death, with his mouth sagging open, his face drained, his dark eyes unfocused.

'I'll bring the horses in!' Kirstie decided, thinking ahead to the point when the chopper would land. Lucky, Moose and Crazy Horse would be driven wild by the noise and by the alarming sight of the monster machine descending from the sky.

'Good thinking.' Lisa hurried to help.

They ran down the row of stalls, out into the open, as the helicopter rose up the mountain and came into view. Hastily untethering the three horses, they led them under the vast tin roof and as far away as possible. Once more, Kirstie noticed the signs of other animals in the vicinity: droppings trodden into the straw, the heavy, stale smell.

But she had no time to wonder about it. The rescue guys from San Luis were bringing the chopper down on the small patch of flat land outside the fence, as Hadley had predicted. The chopper swayed uncertainly and hovered fifty feet from the ground, its blades whirling up a cloud of snow, the fat body of the machine tilting and turning to gain a better position.

'Easy, easy!' Kirstie told Lucky and Moose. Lisa stroked Crazy Horse's neck and rubbed his bony cheek, whispering soothing words into his ear.

The copter had disappeared in a frozen flurry, churning up more snow as it lowered itself still further on to the small plateau. Slowly it tilted and turned, then landed. Its engine cut out and the blades ground to a halt.

Then there were two men in helmets and padded, zip-up suits running into the barn with stretchers and resuscitation equipment; with anti-hypothermia blankets, neck and chest braces, oxygen masks and all the life-saving gear needed to keep Jerry Fraser alive. They yelled orders, asked Hadley for information, strapped monitors on to their patient and prepared to lift him expertly on to a stretcher.

'Good job!' they complimented Kirstie and Lisa as they ran smoothly by, carrying Jerry Fraser with them.

Kirstie left Lucky's side and hurried along with them towards the barn exit. 'Is he gonna be OK?'

'Thanks to you,' the paramedic told her.

Jerry Fraser looked out from beneath a foil blanket, his chest encased in a brace, an oxygen mask around his neck, ready for use if necessary. 'Yeah, thanks!' he whispered. 'I didn't think I was gonna make it out there! Hey, what about my brother?' The sudden thought made

him raise his head in alarm.

Kirstie gave a rapid reply. 'They're taking Ed to hospital right now.'

'You bet!' one of the stretcher carriers confirmed. 'Looks like he broke a leg and crushed a couple of ribs. We'll fill you in once we get you on board!'

Kirstie saw Jerry fall back on to the stretcher. She stopped at the exit and watched the two men lift him into the chopper, saw him say something urgent to the nearest of the two paramedics. The man nodded and came back across.

'He says thanks,' he told her. 'And something about a horse.'

She gasped and stared hard after the disappearing stretcher. 'Joe? I mean, Wildflower?'

'That was the name. It seemed kinda important.' The man was anxious to deliver the message fast and rejoin his team. 'He says he saw the horse hereabouts, and for you not to give up on him.'

Before Kirstie could ask any more questions, he turned and hurried back to the helicopter, whose blades were beginning to turn, slowly at first, but quickly gathering speed. The noise rose and the rotating blades churned up a thick white mist of freezing dust.

Instinctively she ran out on to the plateau of rock and into the cloud of snow. 'Where exactly?' she yelled after the rescue worker. 'Where did he see Joe?'

But her voice was lost in the churn of blades and rumble of the engine. The man hoisted himself up into the belly of the aircraft and the door slid shut.

The message from Jerry Fraser had simply confirmed what Kirstie already knew; she'd seen for herself that Navaho Joe was still in the area. What she needed was solid information; the precise spot where the injured man had seen the lost horse.

But no; the chopper was lifting clear of the ground, the wind created by the blades tearing into her, cutting through her sweatshirt, whipping freezing particles into her face. She must retreat without the one fact she needed.

'You hear that?' Hadley said. He'd come to the wide barn entrance to watch the helicopter depart, and now Lisa had joined him and Kirstie.

'All I can hear is helicopter!' Lisa complained, hands over her ears.

'No, not that.' The old man was listening hard to a noise further away. His head was to one side, his eyes narrowed with concern. He waited for the snow cloud to settle and for the copter to clear the ridge over Elk Pass before he strode out on to the flat piece of rock.

'What?' Kirstie whispered. Now that the rescue team had left, the whole mountain seemed deadly quiet. Inside the barn, the three horses stamped uneasily, then whinnied a reminder that they wanted to be untethered. Out there, under the intense blue sky, in this picture-postcard world of white soaring ridges that curved and rose into evermore distant peaks there was something that seemed to be upsetting Hadley.

'Avalanche!' he murmured, shading his eyes with one hand and turning slowly to the sheer white face behind the barn. 'West of Eagle's Peak. Look!'

The rounded surface of the mountain seemed to split open like a giant eggshell. The lower half of the slope broke away and started to slide; slowly at first then gathering speed.

Kirstie and Lisa froze on the spot, staring up at the cone-shaped peak, wondering which direction the avalanche would take. The mountain's face was rugged, hacked by deep ravines, dissected by streams which would usually tumble and gush over ledges in spectacular waterfalls, but which today were white and frozen.

'Shouldn't we make a run for it?' Lisa whispered, as the slithering, sliding mass of snow gathered speed.

Kirstie held her breath. She heard the distant rumble of the avalanche and had the dizzy sense that nothing in this world would ever be safe again.

'No point,' Hadley grimaced. 'It moves too fast for us to get out of its path. We just gotta hope that it stays that side of Coyote Canyon.'

The girls grabbed on to his words. They followed the track of the snow slide, closed their eyes momentarily as a stand of lodgepole pines disappeared under its huge, rumbling mass. The tall, strong trees simply snapped or bowed as the wall of moving snow smashed against them. One second the hundred-year-old pines were there; the next they were destroyed.

And the avalanche hurtled on, gathering mass, collecting giant boulders and carrying them down the slopes, making them bounce like pebbles, ripping dark holes in the white cliffs, uprooting more trees, choosing the deepest ravines to smash into, to roll through and on again down the mountain.

It roared in their ears, cast snow clouds downwind across half a mile of glacier to the cattle station where they stood. Kirstie breathed in the icy blast and felt her whole being sliced through with terror.

But the avalanche chose a deserted route into the shadowy ravine of Coyote Canyon; a place so remote that human footprints were unknown, and where even the wildlife of the area rarely made their dens. Snow, ice, earth, uprooted trees and boulders slammed into the narrow valley and piled high, thundering to a standstill at last.

For a full minute after it had ended, the three figures of Hadley, Kirstie and Lisa remained still on their ledge of rock, looking across the mountain and down into the wrecked canyon. Then they breathed again.

* * *

'Let's go!' Hadley was up on Moose, forcing his reluctant horse out from under the high barn into the open. He'd wrenched a yellow slicker from his saddle-bag and put it on over his dark blue T-shirt to try to ward off the cold for the homeward ride. Now he sat in the saddle, waiting for Lisa then finally Kirstie to follow him down on to Elk Pass.

Strange, Kirstie thought, how nature could turn the world upside down then return to normal, as if nothing had happened, as if a mountain hadn't moved. She rode Lucky along the row of gloomy stalls, cold to the core and shuddering.

Ahead of her, Lisa reached sunlight and walked Crazy Horse out across the narrow ledge.

For some reason, Lucky stopped. Kirstie clicked her tongue and squeezed his sides. This was unlike him. His head was turned to the far corner, his ears flicked round to listen. She saw Lisa and Crazy Horse pick their way down from the plateau and disappear out of sight. 'C'mon, boy, let's go!'

Again he refused. He'd either seen, or heard, something taking refuge over there; an animal that had crept into the barn during the avalanche perhaps, when their backs were turned.

Deer, coyote . . . mountain lion, bear . . . ? Kirstie ran through the possibilities. She glanced towards the dark corner, her mind still full of the gigantic snowslide, thinking no way did she want Hadley and Lisa to leave her behind.

Lucky felt the shift of her weight as she turned in the saddle. It allowed him to sidestep and to pull his head against the direction of the reins. Stubbornly, he insisted on them going to take a look.

Not a bear, then. Nothing dangerous. Lucky's natural savvy would have warned him to stay away from an animal likely to attack. 'Make this quick!' she whispered to him, giving him his head and letting him approach the hidden corner. There was a stack of straw, and that living-animal stench; a feeling that, yes, there was something in that final stall, furthest away from the wind and snow.

Lucky reached the stall.

Not deer, not elk. Navaho Joe.

He stood full square in the stall, quietly waiting in a mess of soiled straw and hay, his headcollar hanging loose about his lean white face, the frayed rope dangling. *Welcome to my winter home.*

Of course! Kirstie let out a long breath. This was how Joe had survived all these weeks. In between those glimpses of him on Miners' Ridge and Elk Pass, he'd returned here to food and warm bedding, making the best of what he could find, foraging for scraps of hay left behind by the wranglers who had worked the station earlier in the year.

Thin and ragged as before, with the gash across his knee forming a dark scar, there was nothing different about his appearance. But there was some other kind of alteration. She stared at him long and hard, at his high head, his flaring nostrils and tense jaw, and into his deep, frightened eyes.

Fear wasn't a quality she linked with Joe. Pride; yes, and anger too. A fierce will to stay free. But not the terror she read in his gaze now.

'Easy!' she breathed, slipping from the saddle, and approaching slowly. With every step she took into the stall, Joe flinched.

How long had he been in here? Since they'd first laid Jerry Fraser on to the bales of hay? Since the rescue team landed their helicopter? Had its churning blades reminded the Appie of that terrible time with the train? Or since the avalanche had begun and the world had shifted in a mass of tumbling, crushing ice?

'Poor Joe!' she breathed, reaching out her hand. 'You know me, don't you? You trust me!'

The horse quivered at her touch. He breathed out noisily as she took hold of his halter, shook his head but didn't resist.

'. . . Kirstie!' Lisa's thin call sounded as if it came from a long way off down the mountain.

It was impossible to raise her voice and reply; any sudden noise would spook Joe. And in any case, it sounded like there was a wind getting up out there and drowning her friend's anxious voice.

Behind her, Lucky stamped and shifted, then gave a shrill whinny.

No, it wasn't wind. It was more of a rush or a rumble; not the sound a wind would make on the high ridges. Kirstie's hand clutched Joe's headcollar with a tighter grip as she tried to lead him out of the stall.

The rumble grew louder, closer, more huge.

Kirstie was the last to recognise it. As Lucky

reared up under the dark roof and Joe twisted free of her grasp, she realised exactly what it was.

A second avalanche was crashing down from Eagle's Peak, melted by the deadly sun, throwing the mountain on to them, destroying everything in its path.

9

Joe galloped for the exit ahead of Kirstie and Lucky. The dark doorway framed a cloud of snow which had been pushed down the mountain ahead of the main mass. There was no doubt about it; this time the avalanche was heading straight for them.

'Lisa!' Kirstie screamed above the dull roar. Her friend and Hadley were out there in the open, helpless and totally unprotected.

But perhaps that was better than staying in the barn? Wouldn't the weight of the falling glacier simply crush the tin roof and snap the supporting beams like matchsticks? The picture flashed into her head as she raced for the door.

Yes, they had to get out. Kirstie and Lucky flew after Joe through the wide door into the whirling cloud.

Then she couldn't breathe. She sucked in the frozen air and choked, felt the wild force of a wind that ran ahead of the avalanche tear her hat from her head and whip her hair into her eyes. Lucky reared and tried to turn, tossed Kirstie sideways out of the saddle, so that she had to cling on to the reins and be half-dragged along the packed surface of the snow where the rescue helicopter had landed. She felt rather than saw Joe jostle alongside, losing his footing as desperately they tried to return to the shelter of the barn. Then, at the very entrance, she dared to look up at the mountain.

It was breaking up. It was shifting and sliding in hideous slow motion; great blocks of ice grinding down the slopes, tilting and flipping over, slicing through trees, smashing into stacks of timber that flew in the air as if weightless, or else disappeared under a slurry of boulders and filthy snow. The

avalanche travelled at furious speed down the north face of the mountain; closer and closer, enveloping them in its deadly cloud.

A second before it struck, Lucky and Joe stopped fighting and stood stock still.

The sound of sliding, hurtling, crushing blocks of snow engulfed them.

Over their heads, the corrugated roof buckled. Supporting beams splintered and folded in two. Metal and wood crashed down.

Then there was silence.

And total darkness.

As the roof of the barn caved in, Kirstie lost all sense of time and place. Metal sheets showered down on her and the two horses, their sharp edges missing them by inches, stacking up against the strong metal stalls and miraculously forming a guard for them against the force of the avalanche.

She flung herself to the ground, hands over her head, still grasping Lucky's reins and praying that Joe had stayed close by. These sheets of tin were their only hope, leaning as they did against the iron bars of the stall, and creating a rough kind of tent for her to slither into, as the ice and snow kept on coming. The sound deafened her; ice smashing against metal, tons of snow slamming after it, piling on top of them, cutting off all other sound, light and air.

How long did it go on? Seconds? Minutes? A lifetime? Kirstie stretched out her fingers in the blackness after the avalanche. She felt Lucky's warm body next to hers, could hear Joe breathing on her other side. All three still alive.

Alive in a shelter of tin and iron, submerged under who knew how many feet of frozen snow?

Fear gripped her heart and squeezed it anew. The air in the shelter was limited. Some time soon they would run out of oxygen and suffocate.

And it was dark; darker than she'd ever known in her life before. The only way of measuring the space formed by the metal sheets was to crawl the length and breadth of the rough tent-shape, feeling with her fingertips, reaching out to stroke and comfort both Lucky and Joe and to gain some reassurance for herself from their presence.

OK; they were in a space of about twenty feet by ten feet, and only six feet or so high, dipping down to four feet at one end. This meant the horses must have sunk to their knees and were either lying or kneeling on the mixture of straw and snow beneath. Neither seemed injured, and Kirstie took some time to check herself, telling herself that shock might cut off any pain she would otherwise be feeling. But it was obvious she could crawl and crouch; so no bones were broken, it seemed.

Silence. Deep, total silence.

Except for the horses' breathing.

They needed to get out. At least she must find a way of signalling to rescuers when they arrived.

Which would be soon. *Must* be soon. She reached out a trembling hand to Lucky. 'We'll be out of here before you know it!' she whispered.

If she listened hard enough, she could hear the ice melt and begin to drip from the metal sheets – a dull, plopping sound – on to Lucky's saddle.

She could hear the crunch of his teeth against the metal bit, and Joe's hooves pawing feebly at the straw.

After another age, all she could hear was her own breathing.

This was an icy tomb. *Drip-drip-drip* until they ran out of air.

Unless . . . She needed to find a way out. She must get her frozen limbs moving again, crawl up and down their low tunnel, push with all her weight against the metal roof. She reached the end where the roof was highest, raised both hands and shoved.

The corrugated sheet shifted. A shower of snow sprinkled on to her face. This made her heart thud; did it mean she should go on or stop? A roof fall would be the end.

For a few minutes she was pulled this way and that, not knowing what to do. Try again, she decided. The fact that the sheet had moved suggested that the layer of debris resting on top wasn't too thick. Of course, it could be a false hope. There might be another air-pocket just above, and beyond that, several feet of ice and snow bearing down on them. But if she didn't risk a second attempt, she was back to the old problem of limited air supply. So she placed the flat surface of her palms against the sloping roof and pushed.

Once more, the sheet of metal shifted slightly. A fresh shower of icy crystals filtered through a narrow gap. Squinting up, Kirstie glimpsed a faint ray of light.

The sun illuminated the thin layer of opaque snow, turning it translucent yellow. It warmed and melted the surface, sending wet spashes on to her upturned forehead, showing her the way out of the trap.

But still she hesitated. She dared not put all her effort into dislodging the sheet in case it brought a fresh mini-avalanche tumbling into their place of safety, crushing their last small portion of resistance to the terrible event which they'd been caught up in. Should she try yelling for help? Was anyone out there to help her? Or had the disaster which had swept away the cow station devastated Elk Pass and jammed up any possible rescue route? In fact, Kirstie wondered, had Hadley or Lisa been in any position to raise the alarm?

As she stared up at the single shaft of dim light, she could only pray that the answer was yes.

'. . . Kirstie!' A voice yelled.

She'd been praying so hard, she wondered if she'd imagined it. The voice was muffled and dreamlike, calling out in a flat monotone, repeating her name, drawing closer.

'Kirstie! . . . Kirstie! . . . Kirstie, where are you?'

She was crouched under the shaft of light, able to make out Lucky kneeling closest to her, and Navaho Joe lying on his side at the far end of the shelter. The horses' ears and heads were up; they were listening to the voice from the outside world.

'Here!' she called with all her might, her lungs straining, her voice breaking and choking in her dry throat.

Lucky and Joe whinnied loud and clear.

'Over there!' The longed-for voice belonged to Matt. There was a second, lighter voice with him, crying out in fear when its owner recognised fragments of the cow station amongst the debris left behind by the avalanche.

'Lisa!' Kirstie yelled from under the frozen rubble. 'Matt! Get us out of here!'

Once more, the horses set up a prolonged, squealing sound, filling the small space, filtering through to the would-be rescuers.

She heard the faint voices grow louder and kept on yelling.

'Here!' Lisa found her way to the spot where the rescuers should begin to dig. Sharp spades sliced through the heap of snow that covered the metal sheets above Kirstie's head. 'Kirstie, can you hear me?'

'Yes!' she sobbed. She didn't care now that snow was falling as they dug, that it caved in in big chunks and thudded on to her head and shoulders and on to the squealing horses. 'Oh God, Lisa, please get us out of here!'

'Take it easy!' a third, breathless voice warned. It was Charlie, realising that their digging was dislodging the snow and endangering Kirstie and the horses. 'We gotta go in from a different angle!'

'Hurry!' For the first time since the disaster, Kirstie was aware of her whole body trembling.

'Honey, hang on!' A voice faint with fear.

The digging had resumed, and this time the roof was steady. 'Mom?' Again, Kirstie feared she was dreaming.

'Yeah. You're gonna be OK, you hear! We've got a rescue team on its way. All you gotta do is hang on a few more minutes!'

The shovels sliced through the snow and brought light into the shelter; dim at first, growing brighter as they dug deeper, breaking through with a gleam of steel, then a gloved hand reaching in. Kirstie grabbed the hand and clung on for dear life.

10

A major avalanche on Eagle's Peak brought in rescue teams from all over the state of Colorado. They waited on stand-by while journalists flooded in after them, arriving at the Springs and driving out to the mountains in a convoy of Jeeps. The Saturday evening news broadcast film footage of the disaster as a lead story, so that Kirstie, sitting quietly at home with Lisa and her family, saw familiar landmarks on screen.

'That's Miners' Ridge!' Lisa exclaimed as a news-team helicopter flew low over the disaster area. Already recovering from the ordeal, she was ready to bathe in the publicity created by a big news event. 'Hey, and that's Elk Pass. See how bad the avalanche hit!'

'We knew that already.' Kirstie watched the TV with curious detachment. Perhaps this was how delayed shock felt; cut-off, uninvolved, as if the pictures of the aftermath on the mountain had nothing at all to do with her.

She'd been this way since they'd brought her off the devastated slopes. In fact, the second she knew that both Lucky and Navaho Joe had been dug out safe and well, it was as if a circuit in her brain had automatically shut off.

Now she could hardly recall the surge of rescue workers climbing the slope on foot – alien in their bright orange clothing and dark visors – or the practical arrangements that had been made to get Kirstie and the horses down the mountain and back to Half-Moon Ranch.

There had been a lot of loud discussion above the noise of a Denver news-team helicopter hovering overhead. A doctor had arrived to check Kirstie's condition, and a horse-box from Lennie Goodman's place had been promised. But this part was all a blur now; except for the arm of her mom firmly around her shoulder. That, and the faces of the two horses standing side by side. One golden brown with a fair mane, his eye steadfastly on Kirstie. The other white and thin and ghostly, wearing his worn headcollar, content to stay with the palomino and go wherever he went.

'Hey, there's the cow station!' Lisa recognised another shot of the mountain. 'At least, there's where the barn used to be!'

Now it was a mess of broken beams and twisted metal, of snow churned up with logs, mud, branches, rocks. The camera located the spot where Matt and Charlie had dug to save Kirstie's life and lingered for a second or two before sweeping down the valley, following the course of the mighty avalanche which had finally come to rest in Dead Man's Canyon.

But Kirstie was thinking of the straggling homeward procession, as it had scrambled across debris to reach the part of Elk Pass that had been untouched by the disaster. That was where Lennie's horse-box had been waiting, its ramp lowered, its engine turning over quietly.

'C'mon, honey, leave the horses to Lennie,'

Sandy had whispered, anxious to lead her daughter to a nearby ambulance.

'No.' She'd refused point blank to move until she saw first Lucky, then Joe into the box. The Appie had gone in reluctantly; two steps forward, one back. It had been Matt's patience that had paid off as he eased off the lead-rope and let the scared horse take his time. That, and the fact that Lucky had gone in like a dream before him. Joe was learning from the palomino that this was a situation he could trust. In the end, he'd gone smoothly up the ramp and the door had closed behind him.

An end to his freedom.

'Happy now?' Sandy had asked.

There had been tears in Kirstie's eyes, welling up and falling down her cheeks. 'Yes,' she'd sighed. But 'happy' wasn't it. More like relieved. Yet sad for the lost horse. A distressing mix of emotions.

Then, as she'd been led into the ambulance, exhaustion had set in, and that weird feeling that there was an invisible screen between herself and the world.

'Where's Crazy Horse?' she'd asked Lisa as her

friend had stepped into the ambulance with her and Sandy.

'They already took him back home for me. Hey, don't worry, he's fine!' Lisa had sat uneasily on the bench opposite, swaying with the motion of the vehicle over the icy, uneven track.

'And where are Moose and Hadley?' Kirstie had known for ages that there was an important question still to be asked. This had been it, floating into her head as they had eased away from the scene of the near-fatal snowslide.

Sandy had taken her hand and squeezed it gently. 'We got a whole team of rescuers looking for them right now.'

At first the answer hadn't made sense. 'But where are they?' Kirstie had insisted. She'd last seen the old wrangler and his grey horse disappearing from the ledge at Coyote Cow Station, stepping out for home. 'How come they need a search party?'

('Lisa!' Kirstie had screamed as the avalanche hit. She'd instinctively supposed that Hadley could take care of himself . . .)

'. . . Honey, listen to me,' Sandy had answered, Kirstie's hand cupped in hers. The ambulance had lurched and swayed. 'You gotta be brave when I tell you this. Hadley and Moose are missing. They were right in the path of the avalanche and we haven't seen or heard from them since.'

With nightfall the weather began to change. The day's clear skies turned cloudy, misting over the silver moon and deepening the shadows thrown by the aspen trees along Five Mile Creek.

Kirstie stood at her bedroom window, gazing up the valley. Still no news of Hadley.

The journalists and camera crews had returned to Denver and Colorado Springs, and one by one the rescue teams were calling off the search.

'Eagle's Peak Avalanche: One Suspected Fatality' would be the headline in tomorrow's newspapers.

Lisa's mom had driven out to Half-Moon Ranch to collect her daughter and given them the latest news on Ed and Jerry Fraser, now being looked after in Renegade General.

'They're both gonna be fine. They saw on TV that you brought down their lost Appie. Jerry said to tell you that the $500 dollar reward is all yours, Kirstie!'

She'd taken it in slowly, nodded, said a hollow thanks to Bonnie Goodman. *Great*! she'd thought. *$500 for Joe's freedom*. From now on, the beautiful Appaloosa would be busy living the legend for Buckaroos Trading Company on the main street of Mineville. *Really great*.

She stood by her window for a long time, coming to terms with the day's events.

Downstairs, her mom and Matt moved and spoke quietly, as if she was an invalid in bed.

'I'm fine!' she'd kept insisting, convincing the doctor that a trip to the hospital was unnecessary. No bones broken, no ligaments sprained, only the lightest cuts and bruises.

All she needed was to be left alone to get her head around the fact that Hadley and Moose might never return.

The full moon hid behind a gauze of thin cloud as it got to midnight and the house fell quiet.

'Night, Kirstie!' Matt called through the closed bedroom door as he went barefoot along the landing.

Then, 'Night, honey!' The same from her mom. 'Sleep well!'

('Lisa, who had hold of the radio when the

avalanche happened? Was it you or Hadley?' was the last question she'd asked her friend before Bonnie whisked her off to San Luis.

'I gave it to Hadley,' Lisa had told her. 'He was trying to contact the ranch; that was the last I heard.' Her pale face had looked suddenly drained by the memory of the awful moment. 'Why d'you ask?'

'Nothing. Sorry. Look, take care!' She'd turned back on to the porch and disappeared inside the house.)

Hadley was the one with the radio, she thought now. If he'd survived the avalanche, he would have called in with a message. His silence all through the afternoon and evening meant that he was most likely dead.

Feeling empty yet restless, she went softly downstairs and pulled on her boots. Now no one need worry about what the old cowboy would do after he quit his job. That was one problem solved and one way of looking at things; maybe Hadley's way.

Yeah, there was that. He'd gone out in an instant, like a light being turned off. No lingering in some back-street bar with creaking joints, living off whisky and old memories. He'd been in the saddle, on the mountain he loved . . .

Kirstie opened the door and stepped down into the yard. Despite the lack of a clear moon, the snow reflected light and made the whole scene eerily visible; the empty corral with its tethering posts, the dark bulk of the great wooden barn. She made her way towards it, seeking out the comfort of the horses stabled there.

The barn door creaked as it always did. The rows of horses stirred. Many were still awake; Silver Flash, Johnny Mohawk and Jitterbug, the skittish, dainty sorrel. How come they weren't asleep, Kirstie wondered. She went to check Crazy Horse, who was also standing at the door to his stall, poking his ugly-beautiful face out into the aisle as she passed.

'Hey!' she said quietly, stroking and soothing him. He stamped and snorted, then let her go on. 'Hey, Lucky!' she whispered. There was a special pat for her very own palomino, and a handful of oats from the bin nearby.

'You too!' She turned across the aisle to the visitor, Navaho Joe, and offered him some oats.

His rough tongue rasped her palm as he licked up the food.

'. . . Don't you go spoiling that Appie!'

Kirstie spun round in the dark. 'Hadley?'

A light switch clicked, a dim bulb glowed. He stood holding Moose on a short lead-rope, yellow slicker wet with melted snow, black hat pulled down to hide his eyes.

'Hadley!' She flung her arms around him, almost overbalanced him against the big grey horse.

'Easy!' he complained, backing quickly away. 'This arm don't feel too good.'

'Hadley, where did you get to? We thought . . . Why didn't you call us on the radio . . . ? There were guys out there searching for hours . . . I mean, where the hell have you been?'

The old wrangler's right elbow had been crushed by a falling tree branch as the giant snowslide caught him and his horse with its full force. The avalanche had carried them both hundreds of yards, but they'd managed to skate the surface by Hadley hanging on to the fallen tree with one hand and to Moose's reins with the other. They'd slid and bounced with the other debris, out of sight and hearing of the rescue teams who toiled up the mountain. Hadley had taken a bad knock on the head and passed out, though when he came to, he found that his left arm was still crooked through Moose's reins.

'The radio was smashed to a pulp,' he told Sandy, Charlie and Matt once Kirstie had persuaded him into the house and raised everyone from their beds. 'That meant it was down to me to dig Moose's back end out of a snow drift.'

'With a broken elbow!' Kirstie reminded them how difficult it must have been. At this very moment the doctor was on his way from town to tend to Hadley's injuries. 'And no shovel!'

'It ain't broke,' he insisted. 'I just mashed it up a little.'

'Whatever!' Riding on a cloud of total relief, Kirstie hardly heard what he said. 'You try digging a horse the size of Moose out of a drift with no shovel! It took him hours, but he made it in the end!'

'And we're very glad,' Sandy agreed. She'd pulled on some jeans and a jacket over her pyjamas and rushed out to the barn to answer Kirstie's call.

She'd found her head wrangler (missing-presumed-dead) standing there in his yellow slicker, heard him telling them not to make a fuss, and (long speech for Hadley) no, he wasn't buried under twenty feet of snow; he was back home large as life and twice as tired, so for pity's sake just let a man get out of his wet clothes and into a warm bed!

'Not until you come into the house and tell us exactly what happened!' Sandy had told him.

Matt had insisted on calling the doc. Sandy had meanwhile brewed up a mug of hot, sweet tea.

'Go fix up Moose's stall,' Hadley barked an order at Charlie now. 'Put plenty of hay in the old guy's manger, you hear? He's had a hard day; him and me both.'

A week later, Sandy Scott sat at her desk with a stack of mail.

'Replies to my ad in the *San Luis Times*,' she told Matt. 'Twenty-two at the last count.'

'Yeah, but how many sound like they could do the job?' Matt wondered.

Kirstie could hear them discussing the situation

from the swing on the front porch. After the blizzards of early November, a warm front had crept up from New Mexico and brought fall back to the eastern slopes of the Colorado Rockies. So she sat and swung on a sunny Saturday morning, watching Hadley standing outside his bunkhouse with his arm in a sling. Hadley in turn was watching Charlie work in the round pen with Navaho Joe on a long lead.

'Only three or four,' Sandy admitted. 'But then, one will do if it's the right one.'

Creak-creak, creak-creak. The swing needed a spot of oil; it was the sort of job Hadley would usually do in a couple of seconds.

'Y'know, it don't feel right to kick the old guy out,' Matt was saying thoughtfully. 'Sure, he says he wants to quit . . .'

'He does!' Sandy cut in. 'And I agree. After last Saturday, I definitely think he should!'

'But not to kick him out of Half-Moon Ranch,' Kirstie's brother persisted.

Wow, this was Matt being considerate!

'How about we find some place for him to stay?' Sandy flicked through the letters of application. 'Trouble is, we need Hadley's room in the bunkhouse for the new guy.'

A long pause; Matt turning things over in his mind. 'So, Hadley could move out of the bunkhouse and up the hill to Brown Bear Cabin,' he said at last. He rushed on before Sandy could come in with objections. 'So, listen, we'll have two new cabins built by spring, which will bring in extra income from more guests. Brown Bear is our oldest cabin and it's kinda small. We need to spend money on it to bring it up to three star standard.'

'Yeah.' Sandy was listening hard.

Say yes! Kirstie closed her eyes and wished hard. When she opened them again, she saw Hadley strolling across the yard towards the round pen.

'So why not give Brown Bear to Hadley, let him live there as long as he wants? I mean, he's like family, for God's sakes!'

'Hmm.' Sandy pondered for what seemed like an age. 'He's kinda proud. What if this seems like charity?'

Just say yes! Kirstie urged silently. *Creak-creak, creak-creak*, back and forth.

'Then he can do odd jobs,' Matt suggested, his voice lightening as if he'd hit upon a brilliant idea. 'He can fix that darned swing for a start!'

11

'Five hundred dollars!' Jerry Fraser had been discharged from hospital before his older brother and turned up at Half-Moon Ranch next day. He held out the ten fifty dollar bills for Kirstie to take.

Joe was in the corral, groomed to perfection. Now he looked like the classy Appaloosa he was: strong, intelligent, able to go the distance. The background of his smooth coat was milky-white; the brown speckles covering his whole body were the colour of milk chocolate. And, thanks to a week of grooming and good feeding from Kirstie, he was smooth and glossy, his white mane and tail soft as silk.

Kirstie shook her head at the money and stared down at her boots. 'No thanks.'

'Go ahead, take it. If it wasn't for you, Wildflower wouldn't be here!' Jerry thrust the notes at her.

She heard the Appie come up behind, felt him nudge her shoulder. His old fear of being caught and trapped was gone after eight days of good treatment, though Kirstie knew it was mainly her that he trusted. Charlie, for instance, still couldn't get near to put a saddle on him, and it was especially doubtful that he'd react well to the Frasers back home in Mineville. Yet she knew she had to let him go.

'Y'know, I just had me an idea,' Hadley said in his low, slow drawl. He'd been leaning on the corral fence, watching the transaction between Kirstie and Jerry Fraser. Now he strolled lazily across. 'Jerry, what you want for your store is a nice, easy mount. You need a horse that don't spook easy.'

Jerry nodded and gave a tense smile. 'Thanks,

Hadley, we already got Wildflower.'

'Yeah, but he's an Appie,' Hadley drawled.

Kirstie turned to stare at him under the brim of his hat. What was he up to?

'So?' Jerry stretched out a hand to stroke his horse, but withdrew it quickly when Joe snapped at his fingers.

'Appies ain't easy,' Hadley confided. 'Appies got a bit of a temper, see. And they spook real quick.'

Not true, Kirstie knew. Treated well, Appaloosas were among the steadiest, most docile of the Native American breeds.

'Whereas a mount like Moose over there . . .' Hadley nodded across the corral to where stately, dependable Moose stood saddled and ready to go. 'Now, there's a good horse!'

Ready to be retired, like the old wrangler himself; a senior citizen in need of a good home. Kirstie was all too aware that old Moose's days on the ranch were numbered. Then he'd be put out to grass, grow bored, and long for a little action.

'You're saying he'd be a good horse for Buckaroos?' Jerry left the jumpy Appaloosa and walked thoughtfully towards the grey gelding.

'I know he would,' Hadley insisted, giving Kirstie a big, exaggerated wink. 'You take Moose back to Mineville with you and treat him nice, just give him easy work; he'd do real well!'

Together, hiding a smile, he and Kirstie followed the inexperienced businessman.

'And you'd keep the Appie here on the ranch?' Jerry checked the deal.

'Sure,' Kirstie said, catching Hadley's drift and making out she was casual as could be. 'He's pretty wild now, but maybe, just maybe we can put him right in time. Oh, and by the way, you'd get to keep your five hundred dollars.'

'True.' Jerry nodded and thought hard. He patted Moose's neck. Moose obliged with a gentle snicker and a soft nudge against the nervous man's hand.

'I'd like to come and visit the old guy every once in a while,' Hadley mumbled, making it sound as if the deal was already done. 'Now that I quit my job, I got plenty of time on my hands.'

'You quit your job?' Jerry turned in surprise and allowed himself to be led by the arm out of the corral.

'Sure. I'll be staying on here, living up in Brown Bear Cabin . . .'

'Yes!' Kirstie punched the air silently and kissed Moose on the top of his long, grey nose. She ran back to Joe with a wide grin. 'Hadley's gonna be here!' she whispered. Matt's tactic had worked.

'. . . But I'll give you a helping hand with Moose,' he offered generously, walking Jerry across the yard. '. . . One day a week . . . no need to pay me . . . and Moose is a great horse, believe me!'

'You get to stay!' Kirstie told Navaho Joe.

The deal was done. Jerry Fraser had gone home with his five hundred dollars in his back pocket and a promise from Hadley that he personally would truck Moose down to Mineville as soon as the Frasers re-opened Buckaroos Trading Post in the spring.

It was Sunday evening; a quiet sunset glowed along the mountain ridge. Out by Five Mile Creek there was no one but Kirstie and Navaho Joe.

She walked him with a halter and a short lead-rope, letting him get used to the fact that Half-Moon Ranch was to be his home. Crossing the wooden bridge into Red Fox Meadow, she opened the gate, unclipped the rope and let him go.

He had quarter of a mile of flat meadow in front of him, the wooded foothills and the white peaks beyond. A small taste of his old freedom.

The Appie glanced down at Kirstie, then up at the mountains where he had spent those weeks as a lost horse flitting through the forest – a wild horse roaming free. He tossed his head and stamped his foot. *I remember*!

'Go, Joe!' she whispered, wanting him to lope to the distant fence and back again, to show her the magic of his smooth, fluid run.

But he circled round her, lifting his slender legs; one scarred across the knee. He dipped his long white head towards her and danced a circle of complicated steps to show that he wanted to stay. *I'm yours. Take me home.*

HORSES OF HALF-MOON RANCH
Jenny Oldfield

0 340 71616 9	1: WILD HORSES	£3.99	❑
0 340 71617 7	2: RODEO ROCKY	£3.99	❑
0 340 71618 5	3: CRAZY HORSE	£3.99	❑
0 340 71619 3	4: JOHNNY MOHAWK	£3.99	❑
0 340 71620 7	5: MIDNIGHT LADY	£3.99	❑
0 340 71621 5	6: THIRD-TIME LUCKY	£3.99	❑

All Hodder Children's books are available at your local bookshop, or can be ordered direct from the publisher. Just tick the titles you would like and complete the details below. Prices and availability are subject to change without prior notice.

Please enclose a cheque or postal order made payable to *Bookpoint Ltd*, and send to: Hodder Children's Books, 39 Milton Park, Abingdon, OXON OX14 4TD, UK.
Email Address: orders@bookpoint.co.uk

If you would prefer to pay by credit card, our call centre team would be delighted to take your order by telephone. Our direct line *01235 400414* (lines open 9.00 am–6.00 pm Monday to Saturday, 24 hour message answering service). Alternatively you can send a fax on *01235 400454*.

TITLE		FIRST NAME		SURNAME	

ADDRESS	

DAYTIME TEL:		POST CODE	

If you would prefer to pay by credit card, please complete:
Please debit my Visa/Access/Diner's Card/American Express (delete as applicable) card no:

Signature .... Expiry Date: ....

If you would NOT like to receive further information on our products please tick the box. ❑